RESOLUTION OF HAPPINESS

~ ~

ANN M PRATLEY

BY ANN M PRATLEY

Power Moore Investigation Tales
Hoonigan
Resolution of Happiness
Home by the Sea
Tiger in our House

Forbidden Conflicts Series
Amethyst of Youth
Ruby of Law
Diamond of War
Sapphire of Prejudice
Emerald of Wisdom

Freedom of Flight Series
Christian
Brandon
Trinity

Painful Deliverance Series
Painful Deliverance
Darkness of Heart
Friendship of Desire

Golden Desires Series
The Golden Desires
The Golden Supremacy
The Golden Unity

Chisholm Manor Series
Alessandra

CHAPTER 1

The darkness was cold enough to make Fiona Thompson cough after she inhaled sharply upon waking. Known as Flo to her friends, family, and work colleagues, she remained in a sleepy daze for a long moment before her full alertness kicked in.

Stretched out horizontally, Flo became aware of the hardness she was lying on. Another sense told her that she was in an enclosed space. Tentatively, she reached out sideways with both hands. She didn't reach far. At almost the same moment, both hands found the silkiness of a fabric. Pushing her fingers against it, she could feel the padding that lay beyond, and the hardness beyond that. There was no warmth in the fabric or whatever it hid. She suspected that wherever she was - and whatever she was in - there was cold wood to either side of where she lay.

As panic began to set in, Flo forced herself to move her hands once more, this time upwards. There was no surprise in them finding the silkiness of satin, the softness of padding, and the cold solidity of a hard outer shell again. As one last test, she curved her fingers in on her right hand, presented her knuckles to the ceiling of the space she was in, and knocked. At first, there was hardly a sound. When she repeated the movement, she could hear the dull thud that assured her it was wood beyond the pretense of softness.

Her heart heavy with the resolution of what could be happening, she raised both hands and tried to push against the firmness that covered her. Nothing. It didn't move at all. Once again, she tried, this time with as much strength as she could gather. Still nothing. If there was a way for her to escape her confine, that wasn't it.

As her deep fear began to sink in, she felt past her head and then stretched her feet downwards. Whichever way she reached, the result was the same. There was only silky, padded hardness to feel. There was only cool air to breathe. There was only the dark that she could see. Not even a sliver of light entered around her.

Her logical mind began to work. She knew she was in some kind of wooden box. The cold and the dark left her resolved that she was possibly under the ground, buried. Thinking back to two months earlier when she'd attended her grandmother's funeral, her imagination extended to a further possibility. She remembered looking at her grandmother in her coffin. It had been a peaceful scene, despite Flo's fears of seeing the first dead body she'd ever seen in her life. To her surprise, her grandmother had only looked as if she were sleeping. The tranquility of that had been highlighted by the softness of what would be her final home. Silk, ribbon, and lace had surrounded her, providing a level of feminine prettiness that Flo would never have associated with her grandmother, as the staunch woman she had been.

The thoughts of her grandmother produced the onset of tears. Her grandmother's death wasn't any factor in what was presently happening. It did, however, remind Flo of that coffin, and make her wonder if she was now in one herself. Maybe she wasn't even alive. Maybe something unexpected and evil had happened to her, leading to her now being in her present state. Could it be? Was she dead? If so, what possibly could have happened to her?

She breathed in long and deep. Once again, she moved her hands around in silent exploration. No, she couldn't believe she was dead. If she was, she'd surely find a way out in ghost form. She had no beliefs either way about whether spirits existed, or if people sometimes got stuck between life and death, not able to go into the light, or whatever it was that people believed. She'd always respected the beliefs of others. More logical herself, she maintained a quiet unknowing about things she could neither prove nor disprove, and she'd always been quite alright with that.

As she lay where she was, her mind active in ways that ultimately wouldn't matter at all at that moment, the absurdity of what could have happened to her almost made her laugh. How many times since meeting Daniel had her friends and family told her that he wasn't the person she saw him as? How many times had people said that it wasn't going to end well? And just how many times had her best friend, Stacey, joked that she might end up like one of those victims off any of the crime shows they'd often watched together - those poor victims who had been buried alive.

Air thin and panic well set in, Flo began to laugh. She'd been warned about this very scenario. Instead of heeding those warnings, she had persisted in her pride in believing that she was right about Daniel and everyone else was wrong. How she'd argued with them that they didn't know him as she did. They hadn't seen his soft side … his caring side … his *loving* side. Of course, they couldn't see him as she did. They didn't know him. She did - or so she had thought. Maybe that was an illusion too - the biggest illusion of all. Just how well did she even know her husband?

Yes, it was a strange moment to laugh, but still, she did. She let a shrill sound leave her mouth, its pitch high.

That was before Fiona Thompson, better known as Flo, began to truly scream.

CHAPTER 2

"I'm just so lonely!" Flo cried passionately to her closest friends during their monthly dinner date. Stacey, Grant, Toby, and Christine had each expressed at least one opinion so far. Flo suspected that each had far more to say yet about what she'd just told them. That didn't deter her from further making her plea for them to understand. "You guys know that it's been almost two years since Brent and I broke up. I don't know why you're so surprised by this, or why you're making such a big deal about it."

Hearing Flo's voice almost break as she mentioned the name of her ex-boyfriend, Grant moved around the dining table and placed his arms around Flo protectively from behind her chair.

"It's not that you're so eager to meet someone that has us worried, Flo," he said gently as he leaned in, close to her ear. "It's that you're choosing this particular way to meet someone that's the concern," he continued. "There are psychos out there who are using dating apps as a buffet to find their victims."

Flo sighed, then laughed loudly.

"Well, there are psychos *everywhere*," she said. "There always have been. If they're looking for me, they hardly need to sign up to Tinder, Bumble, or any other dating realm to find me, do they!" she exclaimed in exasperation.

She loved her friends, and she appreciated that they, in turn, loved her. It was bittersweet knowing that they meant well, all the while driving her crazy with their over the top attempts to keep her safe. She was 23 years old, after all. Surely that was old enough for everyone to back off and let her live her life, mistakes and all.

Grant hugged her again from where he stood behind her. He could sense the tenseness that emanated through her rigid shoulders. That didn't make him feel good. As always, the four of them had expressed their concern that came with their love for Flo. As always, it seemed to have the exact opposite effect and reaction from her as what they'd expected or intended.

With her back to him, Flo was oblivious to the look Grant gave to the others seated around the table. Knowing him as well as she did, if she'd seen it, she would have accurately interpreted the look as one of intense sadness.

"Well, I think you are very brave, Flo," Toby pitched in. As was usually the case, he was in support of her current venture. Consistently, he was a loyal supporter of anything she attempted. He always had been. It was one of the many things she loved about having him as her long-time friend. "Everyone else is doing it, so why shouldn't you? Don't listen to these old fuddy-duddies. They don't know what they're talking about," he continued as he reached across the table and touched her hand with his. "The best advice I can give you about this online dating lark is to simply be careful. Grant wasn't exaggerating when he said there are nutters out there. Use your common sense, and I have no doubt you'll be perfectly fine."

In response to his passionate words, Christine turned toward him.

"Oh, yeah! You mentioned a while back that *you* were going to do the online dating thing," she said, happy to divert the conversation away from the hard time Flo had been getting. She, too, had expressed her concern, but there always came a time to change the subject. In her opinion, that time had come. "What happened to that? Did you go through with it?" she asked, the mischief-maker in her wanting to push him into defensive mode.

As a group, they didn't get together very often, but when they did, they all had their personality quirks that shone brightly. In general, Christine knew she was the person of the group who understood the concept of 'pushing someone's buttons'. She could push someone enough until they threw up their hands in almost craziness before that person would realize what she'd done and end up laughing with the rest of them.

"Oh, yes, I did," Toby replied as he grinned broadly. "It's like a … hmm, what word did you just use, Grant? Buffet?" he asked, letting loose a loud laugh as he did. After he spoke, he waited, knowing how to bring his friends to the point of desperation in needing to know what he had been up to.

"Well, come on then!" Stacey said in very evident exasperation. "Shit, you're a bugger for only throwing the fishing line out and teasing us with your scant details! What kind of friend are you, always making us beg for information?" she continued, grinning widely.

Toby laughed again as he nodded.

"L-O-L, you! Some things a gentleman never tells," he said as he winked, tapped the side of his nose, and continued to smile. "But I will tell you that since our last catch up, my friends, I did put up a profile, I did get a load of matches, and I did take the plunge and meet seven people in person. Most of them were even normal, I'll have you know."

"*Most* of them were normal?" Grant asked, laughing. "What about the others? Are you implying you met some *abnormal* people in the bunch that you met?"

"Well, yes, actually. A couple were a bit over the top … for me, anyway," Toby said, his voice and face sobering. "One of them I chatted to for a couple of weeks. We got on okay, and to be honest, I was really looking forward to meeting her," he said before pausing for effect. Always one for the dramatic.

"Oh my god! *And??*" Christine asked, exasperation evident in her tone.

"And!" Toby continued, smiling at her before growing serious again. "And then she went a bit loopy. Well, loopy probably isn't the right word. One minute, it seemed like we were just chatting, checking in each day to say hi and have a short conversation before signing off. A couple of times, we tentatively arranged to meet up, but then I had to cancel because of work, and then she had to cancel because of something to do with her kids." He took a moment to contemplate. Everything looked different in hindsight, and even more different when explaining it to others.

"Anyway, I was pretty relaxed about it, but one night she sent me a message asking how my day was, and I didn't reply for a couple of hours," he continued. "By the time I picked up my phone and checked my messages, she'd gone from asking that question to asking where I was and what I was doing, and then into complete interrogation mode. All up, she'd sent 17 messages, each one reading more desperate than the last. The last couple were pretty nasty, saying I'd been purposely leading her on to make her develop feelings for me, without any intention of ever meeting her, let alone having a relationship with her." He paused a moment as he looked around the faces of each of his friends. "It did leave me feeling a little worried about her at first. After that, I just felt pissed off that someone had made an assumption about me that was completely wrong. She'd made it all up in her head. I hadn't even had the chance to respond to the conversation before she'd moved onto the next level of paranoia."

Flo watched his face as he spoke. She didn't particularly like what he was saying, but she was drawn to listen.

"Did you reply in the end?" she asked.

"I did," Toby said. "But only to send a message telling her I was sorry she felt that way, but I sincerely hoped she would find someone more suited to her. I haven't contacted her or heard from her since."

For a moment, Toby wondered if that particular online dater had found someone. He hoped so. He hadn't enjoyed reading someone's words that appeared to have been spoken from lonely desperation.

"Anyway, that freaked me out a little bit but didn't deter me," he continued. "I kept my profile up, kept chatting to people, and just got on with it."

"Okay, but that's only one example of someone acting over the top," Grant said. "What's the other one?"

Toby looked at him and began to speak again.

"One of them found out where I worked and turned up there," he said. "We'd only met one time, and a couple of days had passed without either of us having made contact again. I thought that since I hadn't heard anything, we were both equally uninterested in seeing each other a second time. Unfortunately, that wasn't the case at all."

Flo felt mesmerized by his words. She found herself midway between wanting to know all about other people's online dating experiences, and not wanting to know anything at all.

"What happened then?" she asked tentatively, not sure she should hear the details if she was going to embark on a similar journey as her friend had.

"Well, I don't know really," Toby replied. "I mean, we only messaged in the app. I don't give out my mobile number to anyone before I meet them, and with her, I didn't even give it out *after* I had met her. Even though I did give her my real first name, I never mentioned my last name. I did tell her that I worked in retail, selling menswear, but I specifically didn't say the name of the shop I worked in. I don't have any idea how she found me," he said, thoughtful.

Stacey joined in the conversation, beginning to feel intrigued. Well settled into a four-year relationship with her high school sweetheart, the entire concept of online dating seemed foreign to her.

"Wait! Backtrack," she said. "You met this girl … and … how was the date then? What made you think you didn't want to see her again?"

Toby turned toward her.

"I love how you guys are interested in the dates I've had that haven't been enjoyable, instead of the ones that *have* been," he said with a serious look on his face even though his voice betrayed a slight amusement.

"Toby!" he heard all four of his friends exclaim at once, making him laugh softly.

"Okay, okay!" he replied. "Oh, I mean, at first sight, I could tell that she was the person in the profile I'd seen, but the photos she'd used obviously weren't recent. Why chicks do that, I have no idea. It only makes things extremely uncomfortable when we come face to face," he said before turning to look directly at Flo. "Don't you do that! I can't see it would ever end well for anybody doing the online dating thing!" he continued, pointing at her.

Flo shook her head while trying to maintain a solemn expression on her face.

"I won't, I promise," she said. "Now get on with the story. I need to hear these things before I start meeting people. *If* anybody wants to meet me, that is. I've heard there's no shortage of women who look like models in there. Maybe nobody will even like how I look. I'm just me."

"Don't be silly, Flo," Toby said. "There are women in there who are all shapes, sizes, and ages. I have no doubt whatsoever that you'll be popular. That's exactly why I'm sharing my experience with you. I wouldn't be doing that if I thought you weren't likely to get any matches, would I!"

"Okay, sorry," Flo replied as she smiled at him. "Tell us more about the date itself ... *please*."

"Actually, as far as dates go, it was okay," Toby continued. "We met at Best Café after work, just for a coffee. Like I said, I was a bit surprised by what she looked like. I don't mean she was unattractive or anything, but she'd been pretty stupid to only show old photos. It was obvious that she is older now, and that put me off quite a bit, not because of what she looked like, but because she'd been so dishonest. It's a bit sad really because as she is now, she's quite nice to look at. I can't look past dishonesty, though. It might be different if I just wanted a shag, but I was meeting people with the hope that I might meet someone I'd at least want to date for a while. If someone can't be honest just in the simple act of showing what they currently look like, what else are they likely to lie about?"

Everyone waited patiently as Toby let out a sigh and remained quiet for a moment before continuing.

"Anyway, I endured the date, but all I kept thinking about was that she wasn't who she'd presented herself to be, and that was like a huge red flag being waved at me. After an hour or so of chatting, I made the excuse that I had to get going. Before I left, I thanked her for meeting me and told her I'd enjoyed our chat. I left her at the café doors. She went one way, I went the other, and I really thought that would be that," he said. "That was on a Thursday night. A few mornings later, she walked into my workplace. It was so weird. I mean, she didn't look like she was just strolling around town, looking for clothing and checking out each store. When she walked in, she downright looked as though she knew I was there. She entered and seemed to see me straight away. I didn't even have time to hide out back."

"She can't have been so bad that you had to hide!"

Grant said. "You just said you had an enjoyable date with her!"

"Oh, well, it was alright - like it wasn't *bad*. That didn't mean I wanted to see her again. You know my feelings about honesty," Toby said quietly. "Anyway, she walked up to me, hugged me, and talked a mile a minute, as if she considered me her boyfriend or something. It freaked me out no end!"

Stacey smiled at what seemed like an over exaggeration to her.

"Oh, come on! A girl talks to you, and you assume she thinks you're her boyfriend?" she teased. "Why do guys make that assumption? Man, you guys have one weird paranoia about that stuff. Sometimes a girl is just being *friendly*."

"Yeah, maybe," Toby said. "But her saying that she wanted me to go with her that night to her parents' anniversary dinner still freaked me out. I mean, who asks someone they met only once to go to a family event like that? Come on, that's weird!"

"So what did you do?" Flo asked.

Toby turned to her and gave a sad smile she was well used to seeing.

"I told her that I had enjoyed her conversation, but I didn't feel like I wanted to pursue anything with her," he replied. "Then she burst into tears. No lie! Right there in the middle of the store - my *workplace* - she burst into tears and kept asking why. Why? Why? *Why?* She kept saying it over and over. Bloody hell! I started to freak out myself. All I could do was keep trying to talk to her, telling her she was attractive and would have no trouble meeting someone else, but we weren't right for one another. After a while, she seemed to accept my compliments and calm down. I guess she just needed some validation or something," he said, shrugging his shoulders. "I don't know. It was enough to make me nervous about meeting more people, though. Strange chicks showing up where I work isn't something I want."

"And you have just told Flo that she should do this too? Are you crazy?" Christine asked.

"But that's my point, Christine!" Toby replied. "I met that person, and yes, she freaked me out, but then I met five other people, and they were all great! There was no deception about their photos, or anything off about them at all."

"That you know of," Christine said.

"Yes, that I know of, Miss Negative Nelly," Toby responded, teasing her before he turned to face Flo. "What I learned about that is that it's really good to monitor my conversation to make sure that I'm not giving away any clues that could put me in that situation again from a first date. I still don't know how that woman figured out where I work or what days I work, but I guess I must have given something away that she latched onto. Since then, I've been more careful on the first date, reserving opening up about too much until I see someone a second time."

"So ... you're seeing someone now?" Flo asked tentatively.

"No ... well, maybe?" Toby replied, grinning. "I don't know. Three of the seven I've met, I have seen more than once. I'm happy taking it slow and seeing if I can build a friendship first. They each know that's what I'm doing."

"And they each know that you are seeing *several* people?" Christine asked.

"Oh, yeah, of course. I've made it clear that I want to meet people - plural. I'll keep doing that, just as I expect them to as well," Toby replied before pausing for a moment. "When I've gotten to know someone, and it feels right, I'll happily pull my profile down and not meet anyone else. Right now, it's too early for me to make that call about the women I've met."

He looked at Flo, watching her facial expression and body language. He could tell from their years of friendship that he'd put her into a minor state of worry.

"Flo, you'll be fine," he said to reassure her. "You just need to use your gut instinct and make sure you don't meet anyone while you have your rose-colored glasses on. It's easy to see what we want to see - to imagine a person fitting into our lives exactly how we'd like someone to. It's far better, especially in online dating, to try and keep your sense of reality intact. Being lonely or wanting to find a partner is no reason to be with someone just because they might show they want to be with you. I think lots of people make that mistake. They place far too much importance on whether the other person wants them. They forget that the best and only assessment they need to make is whether that person is right for *them*, not whether *they* are right for the other person."

Flo considered his speech. Throughout their eleven-year friendship, he'd consistently shown his serious side and his caring side. The five of them, as a group, were close, but with Toby, Flo had always felt a slightly stronger bond.

"You've given me a lot to think about, but thanks," she said. "Hearing even just this little bit about your experience makes me see I have to really think about what I'm doing."

"You'll give up this idea then?" Grant asked.

"No, I want to get back into dating, even if just for the sake of building up some confidence in dating itself. But I will be careful, so don't worry about me," Flo replied as she looked around each of the faces she knew and loved so much. "I'm a big girl. I can do this."

"Wow, I feel so old," Christine said. "See, this is exactly why I need you guys and love you so much. I just have to live vicariously through you!"

Grant laughed as he wrapped an arm around Christine's shoulders.

"You're the same age as all of us, silly!" he teased

her.

The five friends laughed. As they did so, Flo felt sadness at the thought that one day they might not all be able to meet up together anymore.

CHAPTER 3

Flo stared at the screen of her mobile phone. 'Enter user login name', the dating app said as it seemed to look right at her, waiting for her response. That, in itself, seemed a huge thing to consider in the moment.

Several days had passed since her catch up with Grant, Christine, Toby, and Stacey. Even though she had decided, before she'd caught up with them, that she would do it, she'd wanted to take her time in mentally preparing to embark on her online dating journey. Of most importance, she'd wanted to take time to consider why she even wanted to do it. Was she lonely? She didn't feel like she was. Sure, she didn't see her best friends very often, but she knew they were always there for her if she needed them, just as she was there for them. Day to day, she had good neighbors in her apartment block, and two older sisters who she saw for brunch at The Black Rock Café every Sunday. That, combined with her job as a writer for the local newspaper, certainly provided her with people in her life.

When she sat down and considered who she was as a person, she accepted that she did like solitude. She'd never been someone who needed people close by all the time. Her ex, Brent, had been well suited to her in that way. They'd had their individual lives away from each other. That had worked well until she'd learned that a fair amount of his 'independent time' had actually been spent with another woman. It was only two years that Flo and Brent had stayed together. He'd been screwing someone else for a quarter of that time. In truth, Flo suspected that maybe he'd been unfaithful the entire time they were seeing each other. She no longer cared if that were the case. Cheating was cheating, no matter how long it went on for.

Brent. Yes, she'd thought he was the one. He'd charmed her so much at the beginning. After a few months of dating, he'd pushed the idea of them getting a place together, so eventually, they had. For one year, they'd dated while living apart. For the second year, they'd jumped in and set up home together. Flo was just glad that they'd agreed to live together at the place he'd lived in since before they'd met. That had made it easy for her to simply move out. The possible alternative of having had to ask him to move out of her place if they had done things that way would have been far more uncomfortable. At least she'd only needed to pack up her meager belongings, hold her head up high, and simply walk out the door.

She could still clearly remember that day. As soon as she'd found out from Christine that she'd seen Brent kissing another woman passionately outside a restaurant, Flo had begun investigating his movements. It had gone against who she was as a person, being so paranoid and not trusting the man she was involved with. She'd hoped Christine had been mistaken. She hadn't been. It had all been true. Flo had gotten the truth out of the woman who had been seen, and then she'd gotten the truth from Brent himself. It had then been logical to pack up and walk away.

That day, she'd walked out of their shared apartment, climbed into her car, and driven to the home of her oldest sister, Kim. Her sister hadn't hesitated in quickly setting up a small bed in the office of her home, insisting Flo could stay as long as she wanted to.

For weeks, Flo had remained in that room, in that bed. She'd had a broken heart. It was the first time in her life that she did feel like her heart was physically breaking. Her chest had ached whenever she'd thought about Brent. In that first month, there had been plenty of times when she'd considered contacting him and asking him - *begging* him - to start over with her again. She never had done it though. Along with her heart breaking, so had their relationship. Brent had done that, not her. He'd proven he didn't love her, and she would never be able to trust him again. That was the core reason why they could never be together.

Two years had passed since then. They'd had no contact for the first year and a half. During that time, they literally never spoke or ever saw each other, even in passing. Then the text messages had started.

At first, the messages had been just of the 'how are you?' variety. Flo hadn't asked why he was messaging her again. With every 'how are you?' she'd received, she had replied politely but briefly. After a few weeks of that, the invitations had begun. He'd said he missed her and wanted to see her. He asked her on dates that she never accepted. He told her he'd made a mistake. She never believed him.

When she'd last heard from him two weeks ago, he'd asked her to consider the two of them rebuilding their relationship. Flo had surprised even herself when she'd so easily replied with a simple, 'Thank you but no. Our time is done. Move on." She hadn't had any response to that, and she was glad. She'd cleansed him from her life two years earlier. There was no aspect of her life in which she ever wanted to go backward. Moving forwards - that was the only direction she wanted to go.

'Enter user login name,' the screen in front of her persisted, patiently waiting. Flo hesitated. Was she absolutely certain that she wanted to put herself out there on the internet for the entire world to be able to see? It was a scary prospect. There was reassurance, however, that at least Toby had sound experience in the online dating process. It was good to consider that she had a male friend she trusted implicitly. It was also good to have a male friend who could offer dating feedback from a man's perspective.

Finally, she began to type. 'FloMo97'. Next, she entered a password. After that came the requirements to enter her gender, say what she was seeking, and finally do the dreaded photo upload. Remembering Toby's stern direction to make sure she only used current photos, she decided to make them as current as she possibly could. Walking around her apartment, she took five photos of herself in various poses, selected them in the app, and clicked 'upload'. It was as easy as that. Painless really. Ten minutes of her life had passed in profile creation and dubious photography. Now she was out there, waiting for an entirely new world of adventure to begin.

Despite what she was doing, she knew she had a great life. There was much to be thankful for. Was she lonely? No, not in the standard sense of the word. Did she want to date again? Yes, she was ready to share her life with someone again. That someone was out there somewhere. All she had to do was find him.

CHAPTER 4

"You're gonna be okay," Flo heard Toby reassure her when she called him an hour before her first date. "Hell, you are going to be *more* than okay. Just keep your primary focus on safety and remember that everything else is just fun. Go with it and don't feel any pressure to do anything you don't want to do."

Flo smiled, even though he couldn't see it.

"Thank you, Toby," she said. "I love and appreciate your friendship so much."

"I know," Toby replied. "Me too. Now stop chatting to me and go pamper yourself. Have fun tonight. If you need to be saved, in any sense of the word, call me, no matter how late it is."

"I will. Thank you," Flo replied before the call was disconnected.

As she stood before the bathroom mirror, staring at her reflection, she briefly wondered if the guy she was meeting would like the look of her. Then she thought about Toby. What was it he'd said to her? That's right - it was important to focus on whether she liked the guy, and *not* focus on whether *he* liked *her*. Yes, that was wise advice that she probably wouldn't have even considered herself. It made sense, though. The person who had to be most pleased with what happened in her life was her - nobody else.

She had just under an hour until she met candidate number one - Tom. Since setting up and activating her profile, she'd matched with 34 men. Of those, she'd unmatched the five who had expressed very blatantly they wanted one-time sex only. At first, she'd felt bad unmatching anyone. It had certainly become progressively easier with each one, and faster too. In her short time of being active in an online dating app, she'd already honed her skills in clicking that little 'unmatch' button.

That left 29 remaining. Of those, 23 had started chatting to her. The other six had remained persistently silent even after Flo had reached out to them. With that situation, it seemed pointless being matched, but she wouldn't unmatch them yet. It just meant she could focus on only 23 conversations instead of 29. There was nothing negative in that.

Tom was the first she was meeting. Although she'd have loved to have considered him the first she *wanted* to meet, in reality, he was just the first guy who had asked her. There were no red flags about him. He seemed perfectly normal and nice. Flo was curious and eager to see if they got on as well in person. Being a writer, she knew how to converse through the written word. She had yet to find out if she could be so eloquent in person with someone who was just a stranger, no matter how many typed words had been exchanged.

In an attempt to relax the feeling of butterflies in her stomach, she smiled at herself in the mirror. She was ready for a new chapter to start in her life. Who was to say that it might not start on that exact night, through the modern-day age of digital matchmaking?

She had to admit, Tom hadn't inspired any particular feelings in her yet. That didn't mean he wouldn't. The possibility was something to smile and be excited about.

Turning away from the mirror, Flo turned on the shower. It was time to move on and see just how much happiness a simple mobile phone app could bring her.

CHAPTER 5

"You're a writer? How come I don't already know this?" Tom asked as they waited for their meal to arrive.

Flo looked closely at him. When she'd arrived at the restaurant, she'd been glad to see Tom was already there, patiently waiting at the building's front door. Punctuality instantly scored points in Flo's view. She was also glad to see that not only did he look like the one photo he had on his profile, but he actually looked better. That was a relief too. Physically, there was nothing to not like about Tom. He was good looking and had a nice physique. It did stand out, though, that the question he'd just asked was the very first question he'd asked about Flo's life. Considering they'd been chatting for a couple of weeks, it stood out like a neon sign.

She took her time in considering how to answer the question. How didn't he know about her passion and her job? Should she just point out that it was because he hadn't asked her? Even as a writer, she couldn't figure out how to say that without sounding like she was insulting or attacking him. After a short time of contemplation, she found a neutral answer that would do.

"I'm much more of a listener than a talker," she said as she smiled at him.

In that instance, she felt the truth that she most likely was meeting Tom just for the sake of meeting someone. He was confident in talking about himself. There didn't seem any particular interest on his side about who she was as a person. A minute later, he proved that theory.

"That's great, 'cause I love talking!" he said and laughed as he twisted the conversation back to be all about him again.

Flo smiled but found herself wishing the food would arrive. It was nice looking at someone who looked like he did. A man so beautiful wanting to wine and dine her was also good for her ego. Unfortunately, his physical shell didn't make up for Flo feeling like there was no common ground between them.

Once the meals were placed in front of them, both ate quickly. Now and then, Tom told a brief story that he obviously found funny. In turn, Flo smiled and forced a small laugh when she felt it was needed. Inside, she only felt sadder. The question flowed through her: would anyone ever be romantically interested in her again?

"Well, thank you for a lovely evening, Flo," she heard Tom say as he placed his napkin over his empty plate. "This has been lovely, and I hope we can do it again soon," he continued as he reached forward and encouraged her hand into his. "You are a very beautiful woman."

Flo felt herself blush before she gently removed her hand and stood up, forcing herself to smile.

"I'll sort this," Tom said as he picked up the little black folder that concealed the amount owed for their meals.

Flo watched him walk to the cashier and pay the bill, just as she put on her coat and slowly walked toward the front door. She was equally happy that she'd been out on a date, and sad that she didn't feel any of the excitement she'd dreamed she might when she met him. On paper, Tom ticked a lot of boxes. For Flo, that meant nothing if there was no chemistry. He just wasn't right for her, or her for him. Sad but true.

"Okay, let's get out of here," she heard his voice say from behind her. As she turned, she saw him give her a truly amazing grin. It only saddened her more. Having an attractive man deliver a smile so grand should have made any woman weak at the knees - except her.

Once outside, Tom turned to her and moved toward placing his arms around her. Flo could sense his hesitation, so moved forward a little herself. At the very least, she could enjoy a hug. She was hopeful there was no way that a simple hug could give mixed signals.

Once she felt his arms enclose her, she closed her eyes and enjoyed the feeling of security that came from such an innocent action, and the smell of a man who took grooming seriously.

"Can I give you a ride home?" Tom asked.

Flo shook her head in reply. Getting into a car with a stranger from the internet? No, that would surely go against Toby's rules of safety.

"Thank you, but I live just around the corner, so I'll walk."

"Oh, would you like me to walk you home then?" he asked.

"No, but thank you. I do appreciate the offer," Flo replied, easing herself away from him. "I have very much enjoyed tonight. Thank you for taking the time to meet up."

She watched as he grinned that beautiful smile again, nodded at her, then turned and began walking in the opposite direction to where she had to go.

Her walk home would take only five minutes from where they had eaten. One of the perfect things about where she lived was the location and the closeness to the center of the town. Generally, she always felt safe when she walked around, even in the evenings.

She increased the speed of her stride. Along her journey, she felt something she'd never felt before. Something was different. Something was off.

That was the very first time that Fiona Thompson - better known as Flo - got an incredibly intense feeling that she was being watched by someone she couldn't see.

CHAPTER 6

"So, how's it going?" Stacey asked Flo when she called a week later. As young as she was, and as happy as she was in her four-year relationship with Mike, she sometimes missed being single. Having two friends who were doing the online dating thing was a new source of intrigue in what she considered her quiet little life.

Flo laughed as she moved her mobile from one ear to the other. Their gossip session had already covered a variety of topics, but it was surprising that Stacey had held off for almost five whole minutes before trying to get to the *real* gossip.

"It's been … umm … *interesting* might be the right word. I'm chatting to a heap of people, but so far, only one has dared to meet me."

"And?" Stacey asked inquisitively.

"Oh, he was nice. I'll show you his photo next time we catch up. He's very attractive," Flo replied, casting her mind back to the night she'd seen Tom.

"So you will be seeing him again then?"

"No, I don't think so," said Flo. "He's not for me."

"But you said he was attractive," Stacey retorted.

"Oh, yeah, to look at, and he *is* interesting, but he showed absolutely no interest in getting to know me. I mean, two weeks of chatting would surely inspire someone to want to know *something* about who they're talking to," Flo replied and then paused. "I enjoyed the night, but it did leave me with the realization that I want to find someone who wants to really know me. Somewhere out there is a guy like that - well, unless I'm meant to be a spinster my entire life, that is."

"Flo!" Stacey exclaimed, her voice a blend of exasperation and amusement. "You aren't going to be a *spinster*. Geez! And besides, I'm pretty sure most people in the *world* are single these days - some, forever. I don't think that word even exists anymore, idiot!"

Flo giggled. She hadn't even given thought to being single for her entire future. She was still matching with new guys each week, and most of the ones she was matched with *were* talking to her. They talked mostly about themselves, admittedly, but it was a start in the right direction towards finding a man she was meant to be with.

"Actually," she said happily. "I have another date tomorrow night."

"Oooh, I want details," Stacey replied. "Name, age, height, length," she said, making Flo laugh out loud. "Okay, maybe not the last one."

"I can only tell you the name and age he has on his profile. According to that, his name is Daniel, and he's 24. Whether those details are real or not, I have no idea. I've decided to not place too much credence on anything anybody says online in case they're just lying. I've had a couple of guys do that already. They say one thing, and then a few days later, they say something that is the absolute opposite. A few times, I've gone back through their messages in case I made a mistake, and it was someone else who said something, but no, some of them are definitely not honest."

"Oh, well, at least you're getting out there and meeting new people," said Stacey. "Between you and Toby, when we all meet up next month, you guys will have *heaps* of gossip to share!"

"We might," Flo agreed. "Hey, I have to get some sleep. I have a deadline lurking tomorrow for a story I've been working on..."

"Yeah? What is it? Can you tell me?"

"No! You know everything I do is top secret," Flo teased. "I'm going to sleep now, Stace. Talk to you soon."

"Ciao!" Stacey said quickly before hanging up.

As Flo lay in her bed, she thought briefly about the following night and the date to come. Daniel. If he looked like his profile photo, he was going to be another looker. Flo had already learned in her first blind date experience that looks did not ensure quality conversation or any kind of feeling that there was a connection with someone. She wondered if Daniel was any more interested in her as a person than Tom had been.

Since meeting Tom, he'd been nice in sending a follow-up message, saying he wanted to see her again but would leave it to her to approach him if and when she would like that. To that message, Flo hadn't responded.

Her mind diverted from her online experiences to her work. She'd been investigating a corporate company regarding claims from a small community that the company had been letting chemicals exit their grounds and enter a stream. Although the highlight of her career was the actual *writing* of reports, it was now her job to assemble her findings and formulate a conclusion from them. She'd never worked on a job with quite so many political implications or general seriousness. In some ways, it made her nervous. In others, it left her excited, wondering if she could do the job good enough for her writing to finally be noticed.

Thinking purely about that, Flo finally fell asleep.

CHAPTER 7

After a tense and somewhat stressful day in her office, Flo switched off from work and focused on the man she was about to meet. Before she'd left home, she'd taken a few minutes to sit down and read through the entire conversation history she'd established with Daniel over the previous week. Even if the guys she spoke to weren't interested in her, she had decided for herself that she would always be polite and she would happily hear whatever they wanted to talk about. If nothing else, she could use the experience to grow her communication skills and self-confidence.

As she rounded the corner to enter the street that the Rainbow Café was on, she saw him immediately. Despite knowing that Tom had been the person in the photo on his profile, Flo had decided to maintain the expectation of that not being true in every case. She was greatly relieved, therefore, to see that Daniel also was the same person as she'd seen on his profile.

"Hello!" she called out to him as she moved closer.

As soon as he saw her and extended the greeting, he began walking the short distance to close the gap between them.

Flo looked at him. He was attractive. Not only that, but he oozed money. That wasn't the type of person she was used to spending time with, but that was okay. It just meant she would hone her communication skills at an even greater level. That, in turn, could only enhance her skills as a writer.

When Daniel reached her, his arms immediately

wrapped around her, and Flo felt his lips against her cheek. As he pulled away, he smiled so broadly that she thought she could see every one of his brilliant white teeth.

"Hello," she said again, consciously forcing her voice to sound confident. She felt intimidated, but she was determined to not let that show.

Together, with unspoken natural comfort, they turned toward the café. Hardly any words were spoken for the few minutes it took to enter, order at the counter, and sit down.

"So, how was your day today, Flo? Did you say you were a writer? Who is that for?" Daniel asked, surprising Flo.

"Oh, I work for one of the local papers," she started to say. She then waited, expecting him to cut her off and seize the conversation to talk about himself. When he didn't do that, she continued. "My day had some challenges in it. I can't give out specific details, but it was something that will affect some lovely people, and that makes the stress of it worthwhile," she replied, knowing her words probably sounded cryptic.

Daniel smiled at her.

"Right! So you are a top-secret spy in disguise as a writer then," he said with amusement in his eyes. "Well, I am okay with that, just so you know," he added with a wink, making her grin. "I know all too well about confidentiality, Flo," he said, his voice sounding more serious. "Worry not. I won't ask you to divulge details. Have you had a good day, though? Did you achieve whatever you wanted to achieve?"

"I did," Flo replied before changing the subject. "But I have also been looking forward to this. It's so nice to meet you in person, Daniel."

"Ditto," he responded quietly. "Now, tell me all about how you came to be a writer. Is that a lifelong passion of yours?"

At that moment, being asked something about herself, Flo felt her heart pick up pace. She knew it was silly. She wasn't even someone who liked talking about herself. She'd just wanted to meet someone who *wanted* to listen to her. It took her a minute or two to shift gears from being a listener to becoming a talker.

The more she spoke, the more she observed the intensity of the attention Daniel was giving her. She couldn't help but be enraptured.

Finally, she'd found someone who simply wanted to know who she was.

CHAPTER 8

Present Day

As she lay helpless in the enclosed space, Flo concluded that screaming was of no use. It felt like she had been exercising her lungs forever. Wherever she was, either there was nobody nearby, or there was somebody who just didn't care to answer her or do anything about whatever was happening to her.

The brief will she'd felt to fight by screaming eventually fell away to leave only resolution in her mind. She was resolved that she was in such a confined space that it was unlikely she would have oxygen for very long. If she wasn't found and let out of the box in however long it took for the oxygen to run out, she would die. In some ways, she hoped that would take less time rather than more. If that was going to be her final resting place, it was much preferred that it take as little time as possible. If she was right in her thought that she was in a coffin, at least she was already taken care of without any cost to her family.

Good old Daniel, her loving husband. He'd seemed such a dream at the start. In hindsight, he might have seemed far too good to be true. What was that saying that Flo had heard in passing many times? If something seems too good to be true, it probably is?

She laughed in a way that was horrific more than comical. Whatever predicament she was in, she was the one person who had played the major part in making it happen. Her life in recent years had been made up of choices *she* had made - nobody else. If she was currently where she was going to see out the remainder of her lifetime, there was no-one else to blame for that. It was all on her.

As she considered that the longer she remained alert, the more likely it was that she might go insane, she let the tears come. She'd always thought herself a good person. She'd also expected to live a long and healthy life, preferably with someone beside her who loved her.

How different life had turned out to be. She hadn't even made it to anywhere near what people considered middle-aged. Although she did think she lived a pretty blessed life, especially compared to so many others, she knew she'd hardly lived at all so far.

Lying still, unable to move more than a few centimeters in any direction, Flo felt a strong need to relieve herself. After considering how embarrassing it would be to do so inside her clothing, she began to laugh again. It was probable that no other person would ever see her again, so what did it matter? When she couldn't hold on any longer, she let herself go, thinking to herself at the time that she'd now probably get nappy rash.

The laughter that emanated from Flo then was hysterical before it faded into weeping of a level that she'd never experienced before.

CHAPTER 9

14 Months Ago

"They are going to love you as much as I do," Daniel said to Flo as they drove towards his parents' home.

They'd been seeing each other for almost ten months. So far, it had been pretty sweet sailing. He seemed to match her perfectly in so many ways, including his appreciation for independence. In that, Flo still held onto residual memory of Brent's interpretation of the word.

Brent had thrown away his relationship with Flo, simply because, to him, being independent had meant he was free to sleep with other people. Now and then, when that memory popped into Flo's mind, she found herself having mini panic attacks due to it. She kept her eyes open, but as far as she could tell, all the times that Daniel had said he was at work, he did appear to be at work. He also didn't seem to be the kind of guy who would settle for only half of a woman's time. If he were to see someone else, that would be the case, and she didn't think he was likely to enjoy that. No, Flo maintained the positive belief that she and Daniel were solid.

As she felt his hand move onto her knee, Flo turned to look at him. He was handsome, he was attentive, and he was everything she could ever have asked for in a partner. Sometimes, though, she wasn't entirely sure if she might be seeing a deeper side to him that might not be so nice. He hadn't shown that side to her yet, if it did even exist. She put it down to her imagination rather than gut feeling.

In their time together so far, he'd met her friends, and

she'd met a few of his. Towards his friends, he had seemed just as he always did. Those social occasions had been fairly easy, overall. His friends seemed to have accepted her without incident. Her friends, on the other hand, weren't so sure about him.

Flo remembered the last time she'd had her monthly catch up with Stacey, Christine, Toby, and Grant. They had all met Daniel several times by then, but on that night, Daniel had needed to attend a meeting so it had been just Flo and her friends, as it had always been in the past. On that night, each of them had presented to her their skepticism about Daniel. There was no concrete evidence about anything, of course. It was all just down to intuition and the feelings each had gotten about the vibe that Daniel gave off when in their presence. Flo had put it down to nervousness on her friends' part. Maybe they each were worried she would turn her back on them if she were in a full-on relationship. That was what she'd thought at first. Over time, the doubts of the four people she trusted implicitly had begun to drill into her. Now she kept her eyes open. She'd also decided to keep a closer eye on her gut feeling.

Realizing they were pulling up the long driveway to Daniel's parents' house, Flo turned her thoughts away from anything negative. For the very first time, she was about to meet the parents of her partner. She should have been worried. Instead, she found herself curious. Maybe someone could hide a dark side from their friends. Would they be able to present the same face to their parents?

"Ready?" she heard Daniel ask as he stopped the car in front of the main entranceway to the grand home.

Flo smiled as she leaned over to kiss him.

"I am," she said when their lips parted.

"Good. Let's do this," Daniel replied before opening his door and climbing out.

Flo remained quiet as he greeted his family, moving

forward only when the introductions were made. She felt out of her comfort zone, meeting parents, and being in the surroundings that she was in. Consciously, she put her doubts and worries aside and instead dedicated herself to firmly listening to all that was said and by whom.

During dinner, she felt a gnawing at her instinct that told her that there was something off about Daniel. He appeared nervous, which seemed odd since he was around the people who had raised him. For a while, Flo wondered if he'd brought her to his parents' home because he did want them to meet her, or because he'd been told to. That consideration weighed heavily on Flo's mind. She didn't want it to. She'd only seen kindness and generosity in all of her interactions with Daniel. It was the opinions of her friends that had planted a seed of doubt, and that wasn't fair.

After dinner, the family moved into the comfortable living room to sit and talk more over coffee. As Flo sat on one sofa with Daniel at her side, she could sense growing agitation emanating from him. His parents seemed oblivious to anything being different. That made her think that maybe how he was presently being, was how he really was. That meant that how he was when he was around her might be an unreal presentation of himself.

Inside her mind, Flo felt her doubt grow. She listened and responded when she needed to. She smiled when it was expected. On the outside, she might have appeared calm and pleasant. On the inside, she was beginning to feel turmoil.

"I can't do this anymore," Daniel said suddenly, standing abruptly from his place on the sofa. "Sorry, Mom, Dad. I have to speak."

Flo watched as he looked at his parents and then turned toward her. Suddenly, she felt impending doom. Logic told her that there was no way he was going to break off their relationship while in front of his parents - was there?

She sat silently and watched things unfold with agonizing slowness. Not registering what was happening, she said nothing as Daniel smiled at her. She said nothing as he knelt on one knee. She said nothing as she saw him pull out a ring box, open it before her and ask her to marry him. It was only when she realized that Daniel, his mother, and his father all had chuckled and seemed to be waiting for some kind of reaction from her that she finally spoke.

"What?" she asked timidly. The previous minute felt like a blur. She wasn't sure what had just happened.

Daniel only grinned at her before speaking again.

"Fiona Flo Thompson, will you do me the honor of becoming my wife?"

Flo sat in shock, her mind jumping from thought to thought. She'd thought he'd been dishonest and that something was off with him. She'd gone so far as to think he was about to break up with her. All along, he'd just been nervous because he was going to propose? She smiled in realization. There was nothing off about Daniel at all. He'd just been nervous. It was nothing more.

"Yes! Of course I will marry you!" she finally exclaimed before jumping up to where he'd once again stood, and into his arms.

Daniel kissed her passionately.

"I love you so much," he said quietly to her as he held her tightly.

"I love you too," Flo replied. She could feel tears coming to her eyes. There was no doubt in her mind that they were due to the combination of happiness and relief. All would be good. Everything *was* good.

CHAPTER 10

"Hey y'all," Flo greeted her best friends at their next monthly meeting. She'd considered telling them one by one about her engagement but had decided it would be far more fun having them all together so she could see their faces when she broke the news.

"Hey yourself," Grant said as she sat down at the table they always sat at. "Toby was just beginning to tell us about a girl he's met," he continued, winking at Flo.

"Oh, really?" Flo asked, looking at Toby and seeing his broad grin. "Come on then. Give us the goss."

For the next ten minutes, Toby shared with his friends all the details about his dating life. Flo watched his face and the way it was animated. It highlighted one thing about Daniel that didn't exactly bother her, but she had started to notice more and more. If there was one thing they were quite different in, it was a sense of humor.

Daniel was loving, kind, and generous, and he was always attentive. As Flo watched and listened to Toby, she became aware of the realization that she and Daniel had never really laughed together. Oh, there had been some amusing moments, but never any real good, hard out laughing, like the kind that she shared with her friends. Was that something to worry about? She hadn't even noticed it was missing from their interactions, so she guessed not. Her friends were good for the moments in life that resulted in hysterical laughter. That was enough.

"And what about you, Fair Flo?" she heard Toby ask

her, breaking her out of her thoughts. "Is Daniel still on the scene, or have you kicked him back to Richville?"

Flo looked at him in surprise. The words hadn't been said with a malicious tone, but the formation of them did sound like there was a seriousness to them.

"Of course I haven't kicked him back to … *anywhere!*" she said in exasperation. "Actually, I have some news that is sort of the opposite."

She kept them in suspense for long enough for Stacey to speak up in frustration.

"Well, what is it??"

Flo laughed softly, taking her time before answering.

"He asked me to marry him," she finally said as she looked from one face to the next. "I'm engaged!"

While she hadn't fully considered the reaction she might get from her friends at such news any time in her life, she was surprised by the silence that ensued.

"What?" Grant asked, his face revealing disbelief.

"I'm getting married," she said. "Well, maybe. I mean, we haven't discussed an actual wedding, but I am engaged. He did ask me to marry him, and I said yes."

"But you've only known him for a few months, Flo," Christine said, adding in her share of negative response. "Are you sure it's what you want?"

Flo looked around them all once again.

"Yes," she said. "Look, I know you all care for me and worry about me, but I love Daniel, and he loves me."

She turned as she heard Toby speak up.

"I didn't know it had gotten that serious," he said. "I mean, I know he's your boyfriend, but now he's your fiancé? What's the rush, Flo?"

"What do you mean?" she asked, beginning to feel annoyed at not one of her friends thinking it might be polite to at least congratulate her.

"It's moved so fast. You are one of the most independent people I know, and you haven't even known him a year. Why are you rushing to the altar?" Toby asked.

"O-M-G," Christine said. "You're pregnant!"

Flo laughed out loud.

"No, I am not pregnant!" she exclaimed before pausing, hoping to see at least one of her friends smile. No smile was to be seen. "I don't understand. Why aren't any of you happy that I have finally found someone who wants to be with me ... someone who wants to spend the rest of their life with me? This is what I've been looking for. Why can't you be happy for me?"

"We are," Grant said, his voice betraying his doubt even though his words sounded more positive. "We are all happy for you, Flo. It's a surprise because it's so soon, but of course we're thrilled that you've found what you were hoping to find. Congratulations."

Flo heard each of her friends echo the word, but it sounded hollow. She'd heard all of them give one protest or another about Daniel the last time they'd met for their monthly catch up. At least they weren't pulling apart her relationship this time around. They weren't being positive, but at least they equally weren't being completely negative either.

CHAPTER 11

One Month Ago

"Two more days until you are Mrs. Sloan," Daniel said to his bride-to-be as they lay in the large bed in his apartment. Holding one another under the blankets, he took her hand in his and kissed it. "Two more days, and you'll be all mine."

Flo watched his face as he spoke.

"I'm already yours, Daniel. We don't need to get married for that to be true," she said quietly. After a pause, she continued, speaking almost in a whisper. "I hope you didn't propose because you thought it was some way to secure me." She said it partly in jest but also partly in wanting to know that wasn't the case. Hearing ongoing doubts from her friends and her sisters about why someone like Daniel Sloan would want to get to the altar so quickly had begun to make Flo question things as well.

Daniel smiled at her. It wasn't one of his happy smiles.

"I don't know why or how, but you enchanted me the moment we met," he said. "My asking you to marry me isn't about securing you in my life. It's more that I just want to be certain that you know how important to me you are."

Flo leaned forward and kissed him gently. "I do."

"I'm excited about you moving in here too, by the way. I've already cleared out half of the dressing room, so there's be plenty of room for you to move your things in there. We can shift things around however you like in

"

the other rooms as well," he said, looking around his bedroom.

"Thank you. It will be nice living here," Flo replied.

Daniel laughed out loud. It was a rare sound that Flo hardly ever heard. She considered that a pity since he sounded his happiest when he laughed like that.

"Let's face it," he said. "You already pretty much live here. It won't be that different for us, except that you'll have all of your stuff here."

Flo silently agreed. For months, she had been spending almost every night with him. There was no reason not to. He had a beautiful apartment that was located close to her work, and in all honesty, she loved sleeping beside him. In so many ways, she considered them a good match, but in the bedroom, they connected in a way that Flo never had with anyone else. Even with Brent, sex had been good and enjoyable, but the connection hadn't been the same as what she felt during lovemaking with Daniel. It wasn't even the mechanics of the act itself. It was beyond that - like they were just meant to be. That was the ultimate belief that kept her from dismissing all negative comments from people she knew when they talked about him. Yes, some things occasionally made her wonder about the depths of Daniel's nature but, overall, it all felt right. She would be mad not to acknowledge that and embrace it.

"I thought I would miss my little apartment if I ever moved out, but I guess I haven't been missing it much at all," she said.

Daniel pulled her close.

"I think that anywhere you are, would always feel like a home, Flo. You have an amazing ability to see the beauty in everything and excitement in all that you do. You are such an inspirational person," he said before kissing her. "I am so happy to have swiped right on you."

Flo laughed. "Me too!"

"Flo," Daniel said, his body tensing. "You got rid of your dating profile, right?" he asked.

Flo pulled far enough away from him so she could look into his eyes.

"That is an odd question to ask two days before we go to the church, Daniel," she said as she felt a strong nervousness flow over her.

"I know, but you've never said, and I deleted my account after we met, so I have no idea…"

"Of course I deleted my profile! I did that after you and I went out a couple of times," she replied, still feeling his tenseness.

"Good, because as much as I love you, that is something I wouldn't accept," Daniel said as he pulled her close again.

Flo's heart began beating faster. Something about the conversation made her nervous.

"*What* exactly wouldn't you accept?" she dared to ask.

"You meeting other men. I want to be the only one in your life now," Daniel replied, his face serious.

"You mean other than Grant and Toby, who you know are two of my closest friends," Flo stated, dread beginning to fall on her.

There was silence for a few moments before Daniel replied.

"Yeah, of course," he said. "I've met them and seen how you interact with them. I know nothing is going on there."

"Daniel, I have men in my life," said Flo. "I have workmates who are men, I have clients who are men, and I have friends who are men. That is as much a part of my life as it is that you have a woman PA, a woman receptionist, and women clients too, I'm sure."

She felt his body relax as he remained silent for a few minutes. She hoped he was processing what she'd said.

Finally, he spoke.

"Yes, I suppose you are right," he said. "I guess it's just that when I look at you, I see someone who is so beautiful and good and kind. I expect that every man, when they look at you, will see how remarkable you are."

"I don't care if every man *does* think any of those things about me. I care about *you*, and you are the only man I want to be with. If that wasn't the case, I wouldn't have even considered accepting your marriage proposal. For me, marriage is for life, and it's about loving someone for that time. I thought you knew how serious I take it," Flo said, concern growing inside of her.

"I do," Daniel said, kissing her forehead softly. "Sorry. Please forget I said anything. It's only my insecurities rising up that makes me want to ask you things that I do know, deep inside, I don't need to ask."

Flo lay still. Her mind was scattered, as was her heart. Until that moment, Daniel had generally remained steadily self-assured as a person. The thought that he had some insecurities could hardly resonate, he presented himself so confidently. Even having heard him say that, it was still difficult for her to believe the truth of it. That was a concern in itself.

The doubts were beginning to mount up.

CHAPTER 12

"Hey, hey, beautiful bride to be!" Christine called out as she and Stacey entered the large bedroom where they would all get ready for the wedding.

Having had it placed on her that she would be getting ready and getting married at the large home of Daniel's parents, Flo had initially been resistant to the idea. Over time, he had convinced her of the positive side of it. It was a beautiful home that could hold the event if it rained. The grounds were so spacious and perfectly manicured that they would be a beautiful setting if the day was nice. There was also the matter of there being enough bedrooms to enable any guests who drank too much, to be able to stay for the entire night without having to drive anywhere.

"Wow, these are some digs," Stacey said as she walked in, looked around, and closed the door behind her. "You are certainly coming up in the world, my friend."

Flo laughed.

"This is his parents' home, not his, but I am glad that we're having the wedding here," she said. "It *is* nice, and it saves having to spend money somewhere else, I guess."

"I have to say, it's pretty nice that they are letting us be here with you for the morning, too," said Christine as she hugged her friend.

"Yeah, I was surprised when Daniel's mother told me she was getting one of the larger rooms organized so that we could get ready in here," said Flo. "There's a bathroom there, and she said the caterers will be bringing up food now and then for us to munch on."

Flo watched as her two friends sat on the luxurious white sofa that faced the large fireplace. Once she was seated on the matching armchair, the questions she'd expected began.

"Flo," Stacey started. "You *are* happy, right? I mean, you haven't just been caught up on a conveyor belt of decisions that have been made by other people."

"Oh no, you don't need to worry about that," Flo replied. "No, ever since the day I met Daniel, I have taken time to look at who he is and how we are, and I know that this is right for me. Thank you for all your support and your concern, but I *am* happy to be marrying him."

A knock on the door broke the moment of seriousness. Flo jumped up and ran to the door. Upon opening it, she saw a caterer standing beside a cart of food.

"Oh, good morning! Please come in," she said as the cart was wheeled in.

"Where would you like me to set this out?"

"We can do that," Flo replied, keen to usher him out the door. "Thank you, but this is fine exactly as it is, right here."

The caterer smiled, nodded, and excused himself, leaving the young women alone again.

"Wow, that is quite some spread!" Stacey said as she walked over to inspect the cart.

Flo laughed softly.

"Dig in," she said. "We've got a few hours to clean this off!"

"Hey, where are your sisters, Flo?" Christine asked. "Are they coming today?"

"Yep, they should both be here in about an hour," Flo replied as she looked at her watch.

As much as Stacey didn't want to keep raining on

Flo's parade, she couldn't hold back her questions.

"And what do they think of Daniel?"

Flo had been prepared for the question for a long time, but didn't want to answer it. The truth was that both of her sisters had met Daniel and expressed the same uncertainty that her friends had. Nothing could be pinpointed. Nothing could be detailed. Nobody could be as perfect as he seemed on the surface. Something just felt off with him. Those were the answers that Flo knew in her head. They weren't what she expressed.

"They like him," she lied blatantly. That was something she never did, especially to her close friends. She felt shame in having done it, but she wanted to just get on with the day - her happy day.

Stacey and Christine both knew Flo well enough to see that she was uncomfortable. They knew she couldn't pull off lying at all. They also knew when she felt ashamed about something she'd done. Loving their friend, neither said anything more even though they both knew she'd just lied to their faces.

CHAPTER 13

"You look so beautiful," Flo heard her friends and sisters exclaim when she was finally in her dress. Strapless and fitting, it suited her body more beautifully than she'd expected any dress to. She wasn't often pleased with what she saw when she looked in the mirror, but the combination of her dress, her makeup, and her hair did make her happy.

She grinned at each of her sisters and friends. Her heart was beating strongly in her chest, her nervousness was so great.

"Thank you. I guess that is what happens when your future mother-in-law brings in professional hairstylists and makeup artists," she said, laughing.

"Flo!" Stacey scolded her. "You'd look beautiful with or without all those people who were here!"

"I agree," Flo heard her oldest sister, Kim, say as she enveloped Flo in a hug. "I am happy for you, baby sister, and I'm so glad that I'm here with you today. I know Mom and Dad are proud of you, even though they aren't here."

At the mention of her parents, Flo felt a tear threaten. No, her parents wouldn't be at her wedding, but all of the other important people in her life would be, and that was something to celebrate.

"Are you ready?" Flo's second oldest sister, Amber, asked. "If you want to back out, there's still time."

Stacey piped up, killing the potential for a serious moment with a joke.

"Yeah, I've seen a lot of things in my life, but so far, I

have not yet seen a runaway bride!"

"And you won't today either, smart ass," Flo said, laughing softly before looking around the faces of the women she loved. "Thank you all for being here today. You don't know how much it means to me."

"Group hug!" Stacey said as she ushered them all into a huddle. "Okay, let's do this!"

On opening the bedroom door, two faces appeared. Toby and Grant both moved forward, looking debonair in their tuxedos.

"Wow, Flo, you look…" Toby said as he glanced at her, eyes moving from head to toe and back again.

"Absolutely stunning," Grant finished. "Ready?" he asked, presenting his arm as the person who would give her away.

Flo nodded, her heart pounding.

"Yep," she replied as she placed her arm through his.

After walking down the staircase, Stacey, Christine, Toby, Kim, and Amber were ushered away through the front door of the large house. A few minutes later, Flo and Grant began to walk slowly forward.

As soon as they were outside, they received the view of white wooden fold-up chairs that were lined up ahead of them. More than a hundred faces turned to look at them, but only one stood out to Flo. At the top of the walkway set up for them stood Daniel. She looked at his face. From the moment she'd met him, he'd openly showed her his winning smile. She remembered at the time wondering if it would be possible for him to smile any wider. As she walked down her wedding aisle, she conceded he could. He looked happy and at ease, seeming as though he wasn't suffering the same heart tremors that she was.

On reaching where her groom stood, Grant removed her hand from his arm and placed it on Daniel's. At that moment, Flo saw a slight hesitation in the magnificent smile. She brushed it aside from her mind, pretending not to have seen it, but at that moment, she saw it clearly. Daniel hadn't accepted Grant as Flo's friend.

Far from it.

CHAPTER 14

"Are you happy, my gorgeous wife?" Daniel asked Flo hours later. They had left all of their friends and family behind at the reception so that the two of them could make their way to a luxury retreat a short distance out of town. It was only for one night, but that was more than enough to make Flo excited about the night to come.

She looked at him as they entered their suite and he closed the door behind them. She liked seeing him smile, and smiling, he certainly was. It was good to see.

"I certainly am, my gorgeous husband," she replied as she stepped up to him. "I am tired, though. Who knew how tiring a wedding could be!"

"I agree, but now I have you all to myself at last," Daniel replied as he chuckled. "What would you like to do?" he asked, suggestion in his eyes.

"Well, first of all, as much as I love this dress, I do find it rather confining," Flo replied, grinning. "Could you help me out of it, please?"

She watched as he lowered his lips to hers, then walked behind her.

"Challenge accepted," he said, making her laugh softly. "Now, how does one get into it?"

The night began with lovemaking. The night ended with lovemaking. The sun coming up in the morning produced the need for even more. As the two of them lay in the large bed, with sun pouring down on them through the vast windows, they held each other close.

"I don't want to move," Flo heard Daniel say as he lay beside her, looking and sounding sated. "I'm not even sure I *can* move," he followed up, making her giggle.

"It *has* been an active night," she said.

"Slightly, but who needs sleep when one can indulge in something so pleasurable, and with one's wife no less," Daniel agreed, grinning.

"Wife," Flo said, trying out the word to hear its sound again. "I guess that's a label that I'll have to get used to, won't I, Husband."

"Indeed you will," Daniel replied as he turned onto his side, facing her. "I'll happily make sure that every man who ever crosses our path knows that you are my wife."

Flo felt a sting in his words but only smiled at him.

"And happily so," she whispered.

"I guess we need to get going soon. I do think I need a bit more sleep before we go, though," Daniel said, already drifting off.

"You do that," Flo said. "I'm going to have a shower and then head down for some breakfast."

When she'd showered and dressed, she stood at the side of the bed and smiled. She liked looking at him when he slept. In that state, he was at peace. She looked closely at his face and found herself having to hold back a chuckle. Even as he slept, his mouth was formed into a smile. On close inspection, she just wasn't a hundred percent sure if it was a smile of happiness or something else.

She moved away from the bed, taking a moment before she walked out the door to turn and look at him one more time. Husband. He was her husband. She'd married him because she loved him and liked the idea of them being married. She didn't know why but the sound of the label prompted in her a slight niggle of uncertainty.

Not liking how she was feeling, she quickly but quietly opened the door, walked out, and gently closed the door behind her.

When she walked into the breakfast room, Flo was greeted and seated before she made her way to the buffet to fill her plate. As she stood over the buffet table, making her selections, she felt a familiar feeling come on. She had felt it on several occasions over the previous year or so. Quickly, she turned around to see who was there that was watching her. She saw nobody who even seemed to be glancing at her. She shrugged it off again, just as she had all the other times. It was a weird feeling, but more than that, it just seemed so real to her. She'd always thought she had good intuition, so it was enough for her to be slightly concerned. She fought to put it down to her being in the unfamiliar setting of the retreat.

After sitting down, eating, and beginning to enjoy a large cup of freshly brewed coffee, she heard Daniel's voice.

"Wow, I think I just had the deepest nap ever," he said as he grinned at her and then leaned down to kiss her. "I'm just going to grab some food, and then we'll get going, huh?"

Flo nodded and smiled.

"That sounds good."

Quietly, she dismissed the feeling she'd had. She often read more into something than what was reality. People told her that all the time. Most likely, her sense of intuition was just off, mixed up in the craziness of the wedding. She supposed, too, that maybe it was just her knowing that Daniel was on his way to have breakfast with her.

She watched him as he filled a plate and poured coffee. Was she happy? Even as she sat in a grand dining room, looking at the man she had just married, she asked that question.

In response, she smiled to herself. She knew that the answer to the question was simply, 'yes'.

CHAPTER 15

"We're going where?" Flo asked Daniel in excited surprise. He'd just told her that they weren't having their honeymoon in his apartment, like he'd let her believe.

He laughed softly at her response.

"Paris, of course," he repeated. "Where else in the world is such a great place for celebrating a marriage?"

"But … but … I haven't planned for this. What does one wear in Paris?" Flo asked, her mind a whirlwind.

Daniel laughed again as he pulled her close and wrapped his arms around her.

"Whatever you like, my beautiful wife," he said. "We don't need to go out to fancy places. I'd be happy to stay in a motel room with you, coming out now and then only to visit the Louvre and maybe some little place I read about called La Closerie des Lilas or something like that…"

"La Closerie des Lilas?? Oh, but that's famous for having been adored by so many authors - Oscar Wilde and Ernest Hemingway both dined there!" Flo exclaimed, excited by the prospect.

"Really?" she heard Daniel ask. When she looked closer at him, she saw a rare cheekiness in his eyes.

"As I am sure you know!" Flo teased him back as he hugged her.

"Yep," he said. "Now, go and pack a bag and grab your passport. We have to be at the airport in an hour."

"But Daniel, I haven't taken time off work," said Flo. "I thought we were going to be here at home, so my boss is expecting me back at work tomorrow."

"Correction," Daniel said, looking pleased with himself. "Your boss *was* expecting you back tomorrow. Now she's expecting you back next Monday. Relax, Flo. It's all sorted. You don't need to even give work a thought for the next five nights."

Flo felt a shadow pass over her happiness. It was the first time Daniel had so blatantly changed something that was related to her, and her alone. She didn't know how she felt about it, but looking at his face, she knew he only had good intentions. That had to count for something.

"Alright," she said quietly before kissing him and then turning away. She was going to Paris. That was something to be happy about, not concerned about.

CHAPTER 16

"I'm pretty exhausted," Flo said to Daniel when they'd checked into their Paris motel. "I don't think I'm up for heading out to see any sights today, Daniel."

"That's okay," Daniel said as he pulled her close. "I'm happy to relax here. We have three full days before we head home. That's enough time to have a look around."

"You really haven't been here before?" Flo asked, surprised.

"No," Daniel replied with a curious look on his face. "You don't believe me?"

"Yeah, of course I do," Flo said. "It's just such a surprise to me."

"Why?" Daniel asked.

"Because your family…" Flo started to say. Thinking about whether it was wise to continue, she stopped her words mid-sentence.

Daniel didn't let it go.

"Because my family … what?" he asked, his face not happy.

Flo instantly regretted having spoken her thoughts out loud. Seeing Daniel's face change to reveal he wasn't pleased with wherever the conversation was going, she wanted to not say anything more. Because she knew from her time with him that he wasn't someone who ever accepted an attempt at changing the subject, she finished her sentence.

"Your family seems so wealthy," she replied. "I just thought that you probably would have seen the whole world, Daniel - nothing more."

Daniel walked up to her. The look he gave as he stared into her eyes was strange to her. She had never seen him look at her like that before. For a moment, she felt scared.

"I thought you were someone who was above seeing or caring about my family's wealth," he said curtly.

"I *don't* care about your family's wealth, Daniel. It was just a comment. I'm sorry if you took offensively. It wasn't my intention," Flo said, maintaining calm in her attempt to calm him down.

As if he was a professional actor, switching from being himself to being a fictional character, Flo saw Daniel's face change. He smiled his beautiful smile and kissed her softly on the lips.

"I know. I was only teasing you," he said.

Flo doubted that was the truth but didn't reply.

"Let's order room service, put on a movie, and just cuddle in bed for the rest of the evening," Daniel continued. "Then we'll be energized to head out and see some sights first thing in the morning."

Flo nodded. "Okay."

The evening passed without any more moments of discomfort. When Flo woke the next morning, she wondered if she'd just misread Daniel's facial expression the night before. As he slept, Flo climbed out of bed and moved to sit on the window seat to gaze outside. She was in Paris. It was one of the cities in the world she'd always wanted to see. As she looked back at the bed, she conceded that being married was something she'd wanted to be. Being in love was something she'd wanted to experience. Really, life had been delivering her exactly what she'd dreamed of for quite a while. That discovery made her think that sooner or later, her happy bubble was going to have to burst.

CHAPTER 17

"Oh my gosh, this is it!" Flo exclaimed excitedly as they stood outside La Closerie des Lilas. "I can't believe I'm going to be dining somewhere that so many famous writers have been! Thank you, thank you, thank you!" she said as she jumped up and down.

Daniel laughed, pulled her close, and kissed her passionately.

"It is my pleasure, Flo," he said. "Let's find a seat."

After sitting and relaxing with their meals, Flo left Daniel at the table so she could take some time to walk around and look at the beautiful building, artwork and photos on the walls. As she walked up to one of the large paintings, she heard a male voice address her from behind.

"Flo? Flo Thompson?"

When she turned around, she saw one of the English teachers she'd had during her days in high school.

"Mr. Brammell!" she said, happy to see a familiar face. "What a lovely surprise! What are you doing in Paris?"

"My wife has always wanted to come to see The City of Light, so I thought I would surprise her with a last-minute trip," he said quietly. "But please call me Tony. School years are over now," he continued as a woman came up from behind him and stood by his side. "Flo, this is my wife, Barbara," he said. "Darling, please let me introduce an old student of mine - Flo Thompson."

"Actually, it's Flo *Sloan* now," Flo heard Daniel's voice state loudly, surprising her. Turning, she watched as he walked up to Tony and held out his hand. "Daniel Sloan. And you are?"

Tony shook Daniel's hand as the two men appeared to look one another up and down.

"Tony Brammell. I taught Flo in high school," he said before remembering the woman next to him. "Oh, and this is my wife, Barbara."

"It is nice to meet you both," Daniel said, placing a firm hand on Flo's arm. "We were just leaving. Enjoy your meals."

Before Flo could say a decent goodbye, she felt herself guided out the front doors of the restaurant. She remained aware of Daniel's hand and the firmness of it on her.

"Did you know he was going to be in Paris?" Daniel asked, turning her to face him. With the question being so unexpected, Flo faltered in replying. That only seemed to annoy Daniel. "Flo, did you *know?*"

"Daniel, what are you talking about?" she asked, confused by his manner. "That was one of my old English teachers, who I haven't seen for years. How would I know he and his wife were coming to Paris? And what does it matter anyway? He's just one of many teachers that I had going through school, as I'm sure you did too. Besides, I could have just as easily run into him at home since we reside in the same town!"

She watched as Daniel composed himself and resurrected his smile once again. He was increasingly revealing himself to be a master of covering up uncomfortable issues with that smile. At first, Flo had loved it. As time passed, she began to enjoy it less and less. That wasn't a good sign, especially since they were only on their honeymoon. Ahead of them was an entire lifetime.

"I'm sorry," said Daniel. "When I saw you talking to another man, I saw red."

"Let's just go back to the motel," Flo said, sighing.

"We can do the Louvre tomorrow, right?" she asked and saw him nod. To his credit, he did look regretful about how he'd acted. That made Flo feel better - a little bit, anyway.

Once back at the motel, Flo tried to forget the incident. As time passed, she knew she couldn't. Finally, she took the lead and brought the issue up again. She'd been ignoring less than perfect signs since she'd met him. She didn't want to do that anymore. It was time to speak and make herself heard.

"Daniel, why don't you trust me with other men?" she asked. "Have you been cheated on before or something?"

Daniel looked at her with the greatest expression of vulnerability Flo had seen on him.

"No, I haven't, but my father was … by my mother," he said as they sat down on the window seat. "I don't know how long it went on for, but I know I was thirteen when it came out in the open. I remember looking at my mother and thinking that she just wasn't the person that I'd thought she was. I was only a child, but I was old enough to know about love and sex, and I knew that married people shouldn't be having sex with other people," he continued and then paused. "I saw how much it hurt my father. I heard him say how much he'd trusted her and felt betrayed by her. I guess it did stick with me." He smiled sadly at her. "This really is a case of 'it's not you, it's me', Flo. My childhood experience in this still haunts me, but it isn't that I don't trust you at all. If that was the case, I wouldn't still be with you, let alone married to you."

Flo listened and didn't say anything. She watched as his hand reached out and took hers. As his fingers caressed hers, she felt a little sorry for him. He was a perfect demonstration of how even people with money could find it difficult to be truly happy.

"I do love you, Flo," Daniel said as he encouraged and held her gaze. "I know I have a serious outlook on life, and I do ask you questions that other people possibly wouldn't, but please don't ever think that I don't love you and want you for my partner for life."

Flo smiled. "I love you too."

CHAPTER 18

With the rest of the Paris getaway having been relatively uneventful as far as Daniel's moods went, Flo was sad to leave and go home. The excitement of the wedding was over. The exotic nature of the honeymoon was over. It was time to get on with regular daily life.

"I do love having you living here full time," Daniel said as he cuddled her in bed on the first workday for both of them following their trip.

"And I love living here," Flo replied before kissing him.

When Daniel pulled away, he looked doubtful.

"You don't regret giving up your own home?"

"It was just an apartment I was renting," Flo replied, laughing softly. "It wasn't home. No, I am very happy to be here with you. It's nice sleeping beside you every night, and waking up beside you every morning."

"I'm glad," Daniel responded. "First day back at work for you. Are you excited?"

At the thought of getting back to her job, Flo felt animated.

"Yes!" she exclaimed. "I am eager to get back into it."

"You don't want to give it up?" Daniel asked, surprising Flo.

Shaking her head, she replied quietly but firmly.

"No, I will keep working," she said. "I love writing too much, and I do like the challenge of the investigative side of it too."

She remained quiet as she watched his face. He

hadn't mentioned anything previously about the possibility of her giving up her work. Flo was curious to see where he was going to take the conversation, if anywhere at all.

After a long while, he spoke.

"But when we have kids?" he asked. "Will you stop working then?"

Flo was surprised by the content of his words. The topic of becoming parents was something they hadn't talked about together at any time. In hindsight, she wondered if they should have. Remaining still and calm, she pondered the idea of becoming a mother. She guessed it was normal that he should expect the two of them to begin a family at some point.

"I hadn't given that any thought. This is the first I've heard you imply that you *want* kids," she said. "Am I interpreting you correctly in thinking that is what you mean? That you do want to have children?"

"Of course!" Daniel replied with conviction in his voice. "I thought that would be a given."

"Well, no, that wasn't 'a given'," Flo said, shaking her head in disbelief. "Plenty of people these days don't have children, Daniel."

She watched as Daniel raised one hand to his face and gently rubbed his closed eyelids.

"Are you telling me that you won't be interested in being the mother of my children, Flo?"

Flo found his choice of words odd in the way he'd asked, but her answer was resolute regardless.

"No, quite the contrary. I think I would love to be a mother, and I also think that you will be a good, loving father," she said and paused as she watched his facial expression change from distress to hope. "I won't be ready for that for a while yet, though, and I don't want us to rush into something that big. I'd rather we were far more settled together as husband and wife, and we take time to properly plan for it."

Daniel nodded, kissed her softly, and then grinned.

"I'm happy to wait ... well, not forever, but a few years if you're more comfortable with that," he said, visually happy at the plan that had tentatively been put in place.

As he leaned in and kissed her again, Flo sensed his passion growing. It was difficult to resist him, but with the return to work pending, she found the strength.

"I have to get out of bed and start getting ready. Don't you dare try and distract me!" she said as she pushed back the bed covers and climbed out.

Looking back at the bed, she saw Daniel laugh.

"I wouldn't dare even try!" he said, appearing infinitely happier than he had been minutes earlier.

CHAPTER 19

"Welcome back!" her boss, Suzy, exclaimed when Flo walked into the manager's office. "Your timing is impeccable, Flo! Please sit down," she said, directing Flo into one of the chairs in front of her desk.

"Thanks. What's been happening?" Flo asked, feeling a blend of both excitement and concern.

"That report you delivered a while back - the one about the corporation that was letting chemicals seep into the waterway near its buildings?"

"Yeah, I remember," Flo acknowledged. "Has something happened?"

"Yes. I have heard that you've ruffled some feathers with it. There's talk of them coming at us with some kind of legal fight," Suzy said with far less of a serious look on her face than Flo expected in the situation being talked about.

"Okay," Flo replied tentatively. "What kind of trouble could I be in?"

"Oh, no! *You* won't be in any trouble," her boss said. "I've received reassurance that the legal team is handling it all, so you don't need to give it any thought at all. I only mentioned it because they might want to speak to you at some point, but as far as I'm concerned, it's a bit of a joke."

"A joke?" Flo asked, alarmed.

"Not the situation with what the company is doing to harm people and the community, of course, but the fight, Flo," said Suzy, smiling. "I do love a good fight! When companies dispute our work, we always get loads of new media attention too, which you know I like. So don't worry about it, but be ready for questions to possibly come your way."

"Okay," Flo replied, her heart racing a bit more than normal. She'd thought the entire investigation and reporting of the situation was over with and finished. She wasn't sure how she felt about it not being closed at all.

"Now, on with something new for you!" Suzy said excitedly before detailing a new reporting job that Flo was to embark upon.

After listening to half an hour of details regarding her new investigation, Flo walked out of her office and into the sunshine. She already knew where to begin and who to speak to. As she exited the building, she became aware of the sunshine beaming down on her. Instead of rushing to where she needed to be, she walked the few meters it took to reach the large water fountain that stood outside the building. There she sat on the edge. Listening to the water gushing down while turning her face to the sun, she felt at peace. She was in a new life with a husband and a new home. She'd just been given a new assignment at work. Everything felt right - until she tuned into her intuition and became aware once more that someone was possibly watching her.

Opening her eyes, she quickly looked around her. As always, there was nobody she could see who was, in turn, watching her. There were plenty of people, but they all looked as though they were just getting on with their daily routines. Nobody looked out of place. Nobody looked familiar. Regardless of how strong the feeling was, it must have been her imagination.

And yet...

CHAPTER 20

That night, Flo met up with Stacey, Grant, Toby, and Christine for their monthly catch up.

"Sooo, tell us all about Paris!" Toby said as they all sat down together.

"It was nice," Flo replied, smiling.

"Nice?" Toby asked, disbelief evident in his tone. "You went to Paris! I'm pretty sure it must have been more than just 'nice'! Come on, give us details!"

"Was everything good, Flo?" Christine asked. "Like, with you and Daniel?"

Flo looked around at all of her friends' faces.

"Yes, honestly, it was a lovely honeymoon," she replied. "I loved Paris, and yes, we got on fine."

Feeling all eyes on her, she felt herself begin to get flustered. *Had* everything about her honeymoon been fine?

"Okay," Grant said. "Now tell us the negatives because that is what you need to talk about if there were any."

Flo took a deep breath. She wanted to talk to her friends about some of the little things that had seemed to upset Daniel when they were away. At the same time, she didn't feel like she should, even though she was with people she'd known for most of her life. She trusted them. Why, then, did it feel like a betrayal to her husband to talk about their marriage?

After several minutes of indecision, she spoke.

"Overall, it was good, but there were a couple of instances where Daniel seemed to get a bit … hmm …

would possessive be the word?"

"Possessive in what way?" Stacey asked.

"There were a few times that I spoke to men in passing," said Flo. "There was nothing in it, but Daniel didn't seem to handle that well. I mean, he did explain why he got upset so easily about me talking to men. I won't share with you why that is, but at least he knows there *is* a reason, and he shared it with me."

Stacey shrugged her shoulders.

"Well, guys can be like that. It doesn't have to be a big deal. When Mike and I started dating, he was crazy jealous of every guy who even just *looked* at me. Even now, he sometimes gives me a certain look if a guy looks my way," she said. "Are you worried about the way Daniel acted?"

Flo considered the question for a while before she answered.

"No, I don't think so. I do love him, and if I had doubts, I wouldn't have married him," she said, then paused. "All couples have moments of uncertainty, right? All of us have experienced them in past relationships, haven't we."

"That is true," Grant said, nodding. "And you know best about your relationship, Flo. We're just a worrying bunch of idiots really, as you well know."

Flo smiled at him and nodded.

"I do, but I appreciate all the worrying you guys do about me. Now it must be time for Toby to fill us in on *his* love life, though," she said as she turned in her seat. "Come on, out with it. Where are you at with all the lovely ladies in your life?"

"Oh, you haven't heard?" Grant asked. "He's finally made a choice. After all this time of jumping in and out of those stupid dating apps, Toby has … a … girlfriend!"

Everyone laughed, especially Toby.

"Really?" Flo asked. "Which one is it? I can't even remember the names of the ones you were talking about last time. I think you were seeing a redhead and a blonde. Am I right?"

Toby grinned happily.

"Yeah, what can I say? I love red hair!"

As meals were placed in front of the five friends, Flo smiled at Toby.

"I am so glad you picked one," she said. "Wow, you must have set a record for the highest number of dates anybody had in that app, huh?"

Toby shrugged his shoulders.

"Yeah, well, you gotta explore all the fish in the ocean before catching the best one."

"Have any of you guys met the lovely lady?" Flo asked Stacey, Grant, and Christine.

"I have," Christine said. "She's so nice. I really liked her. She's far more normal than Toby's past girlfriends."

"I concur!" exclaimed Toby, spluttering as he burst out laughing.

After their meals were finished, the group rose from their table and made their way to the door. As always, they stopped and hugged each other out on the street before parting to go their separate ways.

As Flo left the restaurant, that feeling came over her again. Turning to look around, as always she saw nobody who appeared to be watching her. That feeling had happened so often that she had to convince herself that she was just imagining it. Once more, she told herself that something about her instinct was out of alignment, or she was just getting more paranoid as she was getting older.

Walking into the apartment, she called out to Daniel and was surprised to not hear his voice reply. Out of habit, she pulled her phone from her handbag. Two messages appeared and showed as being from him. They indicated he'd gone to his parents' home for dinner and would soon be on his way home. Thinking nothing of it, Flo put down her phone, showered, and climbed into bed. When she was drifting off, she heard him enter the house and come through to the bedroom.

"Hey, sleepyhead," he said as he sat on the bed beside her and kissed her gently. "Go back to sleep. I'll join you in a minute."

That was the last thing Flo heard before she drifted off into a deep sleep. In her restful state, she didn't even notice the look of unhappiness that had settled upon her husband's face.

CHAPTER 21

On waking the next morning, Flo was surprised to see Daniel already up and sitting on her side of the bed, looking down at her. At first, it startled her. It wasn't something he'd ever done before. It felt out of character for him. Straight away, Flo became alert.

"What is it?" she asked as she sat up, fearful that something might have happened to a friend or one of her sisters. "What's happened?"

The look that Daniel gave her was grave.

"What's happened?" he repeated, the sound of resentment or annoyance evident in his tone. "How about you tell me," he said cryptically.

Flo looked at him, confused. He was obviously unhappy. That wasn't that unusual, but generally, she did usually know what she might have done to cause his mood change. She was oblivious to whatever might have happened that had resulted in the current vibe emanating from her husband.

"You'll have to give me a clue, Daniel. I have no idea what you're referring to, but I can see that something has upset you," Flo said. "What is it?"

She watched him as he, in turn, stared at her face. His eyes darted from her eyes to her lips and back again, over and over. She wondered if he was trying to intimidate her. That wasn't usually his style, but she'd seen that kind of behavior in her ex, Brent. She hadn't identified it at the time, but hindsight was always interesting for seeing things differently.

"I saw you hugging him," Daniel finally said, hurt

written all over his face.

Flo was surprised. "Who?"

"Grant," Daniel said quietly as he continued his intense stare. "I saw the two of you hugging last night."

Flo felt a slight hesitation in wanting to reply. She knew Daniel was perfectly aware of her close friendships with two men. That he was bringing it up yet again and in such a way made her wary. His tone veered toward accusatory.

"And?" she asked without flinching. She'd been happy to change her name, move into his place, and talk about starting a family. There was no way she was going to turn her back on her friends for him. In that, she was firmly resolved.

"And? You don't even try to deny it," Daniel said. Flustered, he stood up and began pacing in front of the bed. "Do I mean so little to you that you are happy to show your feelings toward another man in public?"

"Daniel, you know that Grant is my friend, and yes, I do hug him. So what? I've been doing that for years. Why would I stop now?"

"Because you're married!" Daniel exclaimed, his face becoming red in anger. "You are my *wife!*"

Flo watched him. She'd seen a few of his mood swings. She'd even seen his jealousy. Even so, it still surprised her to see the beginning of rage on his face. That was something he'd kept well hidden until that moment.

Climbing out of bed, she stood in front of him with her head raised high so that they were on more equal footing.

"Why are you angry because I hugged a friend?" she asked, then paused, watching his face. When he didn't instantly reply, she continued. "Alright, then tell me this. Did you also see me hug Toby, and Christine, and Stacey?"

"I saw you hug Grant," Daniel replied. "That was

enough."

"Oh, for Christ's sake," Flo said, feeling surprisingly empowered. "When you met me, you knew that I had four friends who I see every month without fail. You knew two of them were men. You've met them, and you've seen me with them, so you know how well we get on together. And now you think ... what? That I'm having an affair with one of my friends?"

"Are you?" Daniel asked.

Flo looked at him in disbelief as she walked right up to him, presenting her face only inches from his.

"I married you because I love you, and you are the man - the *only* man - that I want to be with. If you can't get past this insane jealousy that you feel when you know I'm in the company of other men, you need to work much harder to try. Now, I have a deadline at work, and I want to get there early so I know it's done and dusted before the weekend. I'm going to have a shower," she said and walked away. She heard no response as she did.

Being in the shower alone was something she'd experienced rarely since she'd moved into Daniel's apartment. Almost every time that she'd made her way to the bathroom to shower, he'd joined her. It felt odd that he wasn't even attempting to go into the bathroom, but also good. The argument hadn't gone on for very long, but it had felt very powerful and incredibly meaningful.

Standing under the water, Flo felt tears come on. It was the first time that she'd felt the need to truly weep since she'd met Daniel. Their time together so far had mostly been happy. It still was, except for that one aspect of his nature that kept showing itself, over and over. If she'd seen his level of jealousy before they'd married, she would have called off the wedding, purely from uncertainty about how his words might convert to actions sooner or later.

She wept openly, not holding back. She was now

married. She still loved him. Of that, she had no doubt. She just had to find a way to reassure him that he was the only man she wanted.

In some ways, she felt sorry for him. He'd been just the right age to be powerfully influenced as part of a household going through emotional turmoil following his mother's affair. The thing that Flo found odd about that was that his parents were still together. They'd worked through it and seemed happy together all these years later. It had caused turmoil at the time, but as a family, they had stayed together and worked through it. Briefly, she wondered if there was something else that made Daniel as insecure as he was when it came to her being around other men. Was there still a story in his life that he hadn't yet shared with her?

Mindful that it was Friday and she had a lot to do at work that day, she reluctantly turned off the shower, dried herself, and got ready to go to the office.

Just before she reached the external door of their apartment, Daniel ran up to her.

"Flo," he started to say.

The response he got was a hand held up, palm facing him.

"Daniel, right now, I need to focus on my job. I feel upset by this constant need of yours for reassurance that I only want to be with you," Flo said quietly. "I have to go and, to be honest, right now I need to switch off from you, take a bit of time, and just focus on me and what I have to achieve today."

Daniel nodded but said nothing. As he watched his wife leave, his head filled with a wide array of thoughts.

CHAPTER 22

Kim and Amber sat inside The Black Rock Cafe, just as they did every Sunday. It was ten minutes past their normal meeting time of 10:30am, but they didn't worry that Flo wasn't there yet. Admittedly, she was usually at least a little bit late. After another 15 minutes had passed, Kim spoke.

"Do you think we should call her?" she asked Amber.

Amber looked at her watch.

"Well, she is usually the last one to get here, but yeah, it's now almost eleven. I do think this is the latest she's been. Surely she would have called if she wasn't coming," she said and paused. "You don't think she's forgotten, do you?"

Kim looked at her sister as if she was speaking in a foreign language.

"How could she?" she asked. "We've met every single Sunday for years! I don't see how she could have forgotten … unless she has her days mixed up for some reason."

"I'm going to call her," Amber said, pulling out her phone. A moment later, she hung up her call attempt. "Straight to voicemail. Maybe that means she's driving. She never answers when she's on the road."

"Yeah, you're right," Kim replied as she nodded. "She's probably going to come around that corner any minute."

Ten minutes later, Flo still hadn't appeared. Amber tried to call again. Once again, it went straight to voicemail. This time, she left a message.

"Hey, little sis," she said. "Kim and I are at the restaurant, wondering where you are. Hurry up, 'cause we're hungry!"

She hung up and looked at her older sister.

"I hope she's okay," she said quietly. "This is a new thing for her."

"It is," Kim agreed. "I mean, she's still relatively newly wed. Maybe she's just been lured into staying in bed this morning."

"Maybe, but she's pretty reliable. I think even if that were the case, Flo would still take a breather to call and tell us she wasn't going to be able to meet us," Amber said. "Do you think we should call Daniel? Do you have his number?"

"No," Kim replied. "I've never thought about asking Flo for it, and she's never offered it. I guess we should have gotten it so that we could contact him in times like this," she said and paused. "I don't know if we should be worried or not."

"Would he call us if something happened?" Amber wondered out loud. "I mean, if she had an accident or something, or if she had to go to the hospital, do you think he'd call us?"

"I don't know. I don't even know if he knows our numbers," Kim said. "Maybe she'll still turn up. Let's order and eat. If she hasn't arrived by the time we've finished our food, let's go over to their place."

"Okay, that's a good plan," Amber agreed.

An hour later, both sisters had grown concerned.

"Right, that's the fourth phone call I've made to her phone," Amber said. "It just keeps going to voicemail. I've left enough messages now. I think we have to assume that she has her phone turned off. The question now is, do we go over there?"

"Yep, but first, let me call a couple of her friends," said Kim. "Their numbers, I *do* have in my phone."

"You do?" Amber asked. "You have the numbers of

Flo's friends but not her husband?"

Kim replied with a look of regret. She hadn't thought to ask for Daniel's number, but maybe she should have.

The first call made was to Christine.

"Hello!" said the voice at the other end of the phone.

"Oh hi, Christine. This is Flo's sister, Kim."

"Hi, Kim! What's up?" Christine asked.

"It's probably nothing, but Amber and I are at our usual place where we meet Flo for brunch on Sundays. She hasn't turned up today. Have you seen her?"

Christine responded immediately, surprise evident in her voice.

"Not this weekend," she said. "I saw her on Thursday night for our monthly get together. She didn't mention that she was doing anything this weekend, but then the conversation was centered more around this thing with Daniel getting jealous a lot."

"He gets jealous? Flo never mentioned that," Kim replied. "Maybe that isn't something she wants to share with us, though."

"Yeah, maybe. She does get a bit defensive about it," Christine said. "But let me call around the other guys and see if they've heard from her, or know what she's up to. I'll call you back in a few minutes if that suits you."

"Yes, please," Kim replied. "We just want to be sure she's okay."

"No problem. Chat in a few mins," Christine said before ending the call.

Amber had watched her sister's face during the phone call.

"No luck?" she asked.

"No, but Christine's going to call around and see if anybody has seen or heard from Flo," Kim said before pausing. "I am beginning to feel a bit worried now. This isn't like her."

"I know, but let's see what comes back from her friends," Amber replied.

A few minutes later, Kim's phone rang.

"Christine?" she asked.

"Yeah, sorry, but nobody has heard from her since Thursday night, and none of us can remember her mentioning she was going away anywhere or doing anything in particular," Christine said. "She did mention she had something going on at work that she needed to be in form for on Friday, so I guess you could try her workplace. With it being a newspaper, I guess there's a chance they're open on Sundays, but I'm not sure."

"Okay, I'll do that. Thanks, Christine," Kim said. Just as she was about to hang up, she heard Christine's voice once more.

"Will you please ring me and let me know when you hear from her or see her? We're all a bit worried now too. I'll keep trying to call her, but if you could let me know of any news, I'd really appreciate it."

"I will," Kim said. "If you could do the same, that would be great."

"Sure thing," Christine said.

Once the call was disconnected, Kim looked at Amber.

"None of them have heard from her."

"What do we do now?" Amber asked. Inside, she felt dread about possibilities. She'd not liked Daniel much when she'd met him, but she'd accepted that Flo did seem happy with him. There didn't appear to be any problems visible on the outside as far as the marriage went.

"Well," Kim replied as she looked at her watch. "It's now an hour and a half past when she'd normally be here. Her friends haven't seen or heard from her, but I think they only see each other every few weeks anyway, so that might not be an indication of anything." She took a moment to consider possibilities. "I guess we have three options. We can go to their apartment, we can just keep calling and hope she picks up at some stage, or we can do nothing."

"Well, I don't like the idea of doing nothing," Amber said. "What about her work?"

"Yes! Christine did say that Flo was working on something that needed to be finished by Friday. She didn't know if they would be open today, being Sunday."

"Alright, well, why don't we call by there first and see if anyone's there," suggested Amber. "If they are, at the very least, maybe they can tell us if she's been in there this morning."

"Okay, let's do that," Kim agreed as she stood up. "Do you want to go in separate cars now, or come with me and I'll drop you back here later?"

"I'll come with you," Amber replied. "The car's in the free parking zone. It'll be fine where it is."

Pulling up to the newspaper premises, it was evident that they were closed.

"I guess newspapers don't need to be open today," Amber said quietly. "But then, how do they get ready for the Monday release?" she asked out of curiosity.

"Maybe they just aren't open on the outside now," Kim suggested as she shrugged her shoulders. "Perhaps people are working in there, or maybe they start later on and work through the night."

"Hmm, maybe. I'm pretty sure that Flo works normal hours, though, doesn't she?" Amber asked.

"Yeah, she's never mentioned out of hours work to me before, or working weekends," Kim replied. "So, go to the apartment? What do you think? I've never turned up there uninvited."

"Me neither, but I think doing so today is justified," said Amber. "If she's there, she won't care that we've turned up unannounced, and if Daniel doesn't like it, tough luck. She's our sister, and we can see her whenever we like."

As they pulled up to the apartment complex, she tried one more time to call Flo.

"No harm in trying, right?" The result was the same. "Still not answering. Okay, let's go in then."

They entered the large lobby. Catering to high-end tenants, it had been designed to look immaculate at all times. No expense had been spared, especially when it came to the glorious crystal chandeliers that hung at perfectly symmetrical points over the broad ceiling.

"Isn't there meant to be a doorman here?" Kim asked as they walked further in and headed toward the elevators.

"I don't know," Amber replied. "I've only been here once, and that was with Flo. I can't remember if there was someone there to let us in or not."

"I think we probably need a key card to do this, but we may as well try, I guess. Nineteenth floor?" Kim asked when they entered the elevator.

"Yeah, I think so," Amber replied. "Geez, we don't know much about our sister as far as the normal day to day stuff goes, do we."

Kim agreed but said nothing. Inside the elevator, she pushed 19. To her surprise, the elevator closed its doors and immediately began its ascent.

"I guess security isn't as tight in here as I'd expected it to be," Kim commented as they exited the elevator.

Upon walking to the apartment door, both were uncertain if they'd remembered correctly which one it was.

"They all look the same, but, hey, if they don't live at this one, maybe the people who do will be able to redirect us," Amber said. She didn't feel confident that people in such a place would know their neighbors, but she wanted to sound positive for her sister.

Kim knocked quietly. There was no answer. After she knocked louder a second time, she heard footsteps approach the door, then the sound of the latch being unsecured. When the door opened, both sisters were surprised. In front of them stood Daniel. His eyes were so red that he'd clearly been crying, and not for just a short time.

"Hi?" he asked, confusion in his voice. "I … I wasn't expecting you," he said as he rubbed his eyes.

"Umm," Amber started to say. "Is Flo home?"

Daniel looked even more confused.

"No," he replied, shaking his head. "Isn't she staying with one of you?"

Kim looked at Amber as confusion turned to utter concern.

"Why would she be staying with one of us?" Amber asked. "She does live here, doesn't she? With you?"

Daniel began to look increasingly alert and less sad by the minute.

"Of course she does, but I haven't seen her since an argument we had on Friday," he said. "I thought she'd probably gone off to take some time out. If she isn't with either of you then … where is she?"

"That's what we want to find out. Can we come in?" Kim asked tentatively. She felt a little disturbed by the state of her youngest sister's husband, but something made her want to see inside the apartment.

"Yeah," Daniel said as he moved aside to allow the two sisters in. "Sorry, I'm confused. Please take a seat."

Kim and Amber both sat down, looking around as they did. In front of them, Daniel started pacing.

"I asked her about him. She said they were just friends. That must be where she is … with him," he started to say.

"With … who?" Kim asked.

"That guy she says is her friend - Grant," Daniel replied. "I saw them hugging the other night, and I confronted her about it, but she denied anything was going on. The way she reacted to my bringing up the subject, though!"

Amber watched her brother-in-law. He seemed highly agitated, and more than a little bit weird.

"Wait. Are you saying you accused our sister of cheating on you?" she asked. "Seriously? *Flo?* How ... why would you think that she would do something like that?"

"I don't know," Daniel replied. "No, I didn't think so, but then I saw them, and she didn't say she would stay away from him…"

"Of course she wouldn't say that!" Kim exclaimed in disbelief. "She has been a part of that tight group of friends right throughout her school years. They've grown up together. Daniel, if you told her that you didn't want her to see her friends, that's ... that's just wrong!"

"I know!" Daniel replied as he sat down. "I see that now, but I was so hurt by it that I started that argument, and then she didn't come home that night."

Kim stood and walked to the window.

"Well, we've talked to Christine, who is part of that group. She spoke to everyone. Nobody has seen or heard from Flo since their dinner on Thursday night. That's more than 48 hours ago," she said before turning to face him. "Why haven't you reported her missing?"

"Missing?" Daniel asked, looking horrified at the suggestion. "No, she's just with one of her friends ... or family."

"No, Daniel, *we* are her only family, and we've checked with her friends," Amber said as she felt desperation take over her system. "Where is she?" All were quiet for a few minutes until Amber spoke again. "Did she leave some kind of note for you? Message you? Leave a phone message? Anything?"

"No, I haven't heard anything from her," Daniel replied.

"We need to call the cops," Kim said as she pulled out her phone. Before she dialed, she looked at Daniel again. "Unless there is anywhere else that you think she would go?"

"No. Apart from here, work, and catching up with

you two or her friends, I don't know where else she goes. She did talk about work that morning. I think she talked about some big investigation she'd been working on and had to do some finishing work on," Daniel said. "But in response to your question, no, there's nowhere else that I know of that she might go."

Kim didn't hesitate any longer. Within a few minutes, the call had been made to the police to report Flo's disappearance. Within two hours, statements had been taken from Kim, Amber, and Daniel. Statements were followed up with reassurances that local authorities would do all they could to find their missing loved one. When that was all that could be done at that moment by law enforcement and Flo's sisters, Daniel became impatient.

"Who are you calling?" Kim asked him quietly as he pulled out his phone after their statements had been taken.

"I know someone in the Bureau of Investigation. Maybe they can help," Daniel replied before turning his back on the sisters and proceeding to speak into his phone. A few minutes later, he turned back to face them once again. "They couldn't promise anything, but my friend is going to see if there's anyone there who can help us."

"Well, the cops are already onto it," Amber said.

"I know, but they're always so busy with crime," Daniel said, nodding. "I … I just want us to explore every avenue."

Kim looked at Daniel. "You don't think…"

"I don't think anything, Kim," Daniel replied. "You have to admit, though, this is out of the ordinary for Flo. Why would she take off like this and not say anything to anyone? Even if she was downright pissed at me for being a shit of a husband, she wouldn't turn away and hide from *you*."

"You think you've been a shit of a husband?" Amber

asked, that being the only portion of his impassioned speech that had stood out to her

"Yes. I love her so much, but I say … stupid things sometimes," Daniel said quietly. "The last time I saw her, I was stupidly jealous, and we argued. I felt angry, and she was upset too. As soon as she'd left, I felt bad. I tried calling her to apologize, but she didn't return any of my calls."

"Well, Daniel, I don't care about your stupid jealousy, or your arguments with our sister. Flo is missing, so stop feeling sorry for yourself and start thinking about where she might have gone," Amber said forcefully. She'd tried so much to like her brother-in-law for Flo's sake, but as she sat in his presence, she increasingly felt like punching him in the face.

"We've already been over this!" Daniel exclaimed loudly.

On his face was the beginning of what looked like anger. Neither sister liked the look of that.

"Okay," Kim said, holding up her hands with determination to calm him down. "I think Amber and I should go and talk to Flo's friends."

"The cops will do that," Daniel said.

"I'm sure they will, but in the meantime, *we* are going to," said Kim as she gathered up her purse and indicated to Amber to join her. "If you hear anything, please let us know."

Daniel watched as the sisters began to walk out.

"You're leaving? You don't have to," he said. Desperation was written all over his face.

"Yeah, we do," Amber said. A small part of her felt sorry for her baby sister's husband. Another part of her felt angry and untrusting of him. "Oh, and just in case you don't have them already, here are our phone numbers," she continued as she handed him a piece of paper. "Please do call us if you hear anything, Daniel. I know she's your wife, but she's also our sister."

She watched as Daniel nodded but said nothing more.

After Kim and Amber had entered the elevator and the doors had closed, Kim let out an audible sigh.

"There's something weird about him, huh," Amber said.

In response, Kim nod.

"You ain't wrong there."

CHAPTER 23

When she became conscious again, Flo felt disheartened. She'd hoped that she had been having a bad nightmare and would wake up feeling her usual self after a deep sleep. Alternatively, she'd hoped she just wouldn't wake up at all. To be awake, feeling the damp cold, and being in complete darkness, felt debilitating. She wanted to go back to sleep and wait for time to pass so she would quietly fall into her final sleep that would last forever.

Trying to make sleep come proved difficult. She tried to move her limbs a little bit to get the circulation going. She expected to be much stiffer than she was. When she thought about that, she realized that she also seemed to be much drier than she would have expected to be. It hadn't seemed like a dream when she'd relieved herself. How could she be dry already? Just how long had she been asleep? And why didn't she have any noticeable rash from toileting inside her clothing? She remembered when she'd gone camping once, she just hadn't wiped herself properly and she'd had a raw and painful rash appear. All in all, it was just weird.

To try and relieve her increasing stress, she cast her mind away from the logical analysis of her current situation and focused on her life to date. She was twenty-five years old. Day to day, she felt mature, but she knew that she still had a lot of growing up to do. Would she get to do that now? She suspected not. There was no way for her to know how much time had passed since she'd been put into the box, but she did know that generally her body clock was pretty well set. She'd woken up three times. There was a chance she'd been in there three days and three nights.

Three days. That was the length of time she'd heard humans would die after if they hadn't had water. Calculations continued in her head. If it took three days of no water to die, surely that meant that she hadn't been in the box for three days yet. Either that, or she was living some kind of miracle that was keeping her alive when it was actually time to move on to the next life.

With a new burst of energy, she knocked on the wood around her again. She knocked, she punched, and with as little room to move as she had, she kicked. Then she started to scream once more. If she was about to die, she may as well do it with a sore throat or damaged vocal cords.

She screamed and screamed. As she did so, she was unaware that all the while, she was inhaling the lightest gas that was entering her confined space.

Very soon, Flo Thompson felt herself growing more and more tired.

Flo Thompson then became silent once again.

CHAPTER 24

"Power and Moore!" Special Agents Ashley Power and Tim Moore heard their supervisor, Sarah Johnson, call out to them as they walked past her office.

As Ashley and Tim entered the office, they were greeted by the normal serious tone of the woman before them.

"Sit down," Sarah said, demanding immediate action, as always. Once the two Special Agents were seated, she continued. "I have an investigation for you. This is a bit off the books, but I expect it'll only take a couple of days of your time, so I know you both will want to do it."

Tim looked at Ashley and grinned before looking back at their boss.

"We will?" he asked. He half hoped that he would receive a smile from their supervisor. As always, there was no smiling to be had.

"Yes, you two like cases that are just a little bit different, and this one is. A young woman has disappeared."

Ashley was surprised and it showed in her voice as she spoke.

"A missing person case? Are the local police not involved in that one?"

"They are," Sarah said as she nodded. "But let's just say that what I am asking you two to do is a little bit above and beyond for a friend of a friend. The husband reached out to a colleague of mine who, of course, can't do anything, given their friendship. That colleague has, therefore, asked me if I have anyone who might be willing to do this as a little favor. I told him that I had the two most perfect agents for the job," she said and paused as she watched their faces. "Are you interested? It'll mean traveling three hours north."

"Is that three hours north … by plane?" Tim asked, hopeful they might be heading somewhere exotic.

"Three hours north … in your car!"

Ashley looked at Tim and chuckled softly. They had been partners on a growing number of cases. She never tired of his slight cheekiness, his sense of humor, or his way of trying to get other people to bend to his will.

Tim smiled back at her. He didn't care where they were going. He loved his work, and he loved it even more with Ashley as his partner. They worked well together. She was also hot as hell to look at. He'd had a soft spot for her for ages. Holding onto the hope that one day she would reciprocate his feelings, he just had to be patient.

"When do you want us to leave?" Ashley asked. In response, a file was handed to her.

"As soon as the two of you can get organized," Sarah replied. "In there is all that I've been sent. The request was only made a few hours ago, so everything is current, as far as I'm aware."

Ashley opened the file and speed-read the front page. There wasn't too much to go on. At first glance, it seemed like a normal missing person case.

"Start with the husband?" she asked out loud.

"You could," Sarah replied as she nodded. "Be mindful that he was the one who asked for our help. That could mean that he has nothing to do with it…"

Tim spoke up. "Or it could mean that he has *everything* to do with it, and he's going to work hard to try and guide us off the scent."

Their supervisor nodded again.

"My thoughts exactly. Keep a completely open mind where he's concerned. I suspect that he's either all out or he's all in," she said. "But you two are among my best agents, so I know you'll figure out where this missing woman is."

"Hopefully before it's too late," Ashley said quietly.

"Yes, so why are you still sitting here?" Sarah asked. "Be gone with you!" she added in a dramatic tone.

Tim and Ashley said nothing more until they were outside of the office again.

"Separate cars to our homes to get sorted and then I'll pick you up in mine?" Tim asked.

Ashley laughed.

"Not a chance," she said. "You know we always take my car."

"Exactly. Does the lady not wish to be chauffeured in a chariot to her desired destination?" Tim asked, his face full of mischievous delight.

"Nice try, Special Agent Timothy Moore, but I'm driving. That applies to today and *every* day that we do cases together," Ashley responded, making Tim smile more.

"Worth a try," he said as they opened the outer building doors. "See you at mine in 40 minutes."

"Yep," Ashley replied. Already she was hyped up. She always was when she was given a new case to work on. She didn't care what the case was. Everything ended up proving interesting in some way.

She was happy to be working with Tim again. They didn't work every case together, but they had been assigned to the same jobs with increasing frequency lately. From start to finish, they did work together incredibly well. With her being an extremely analytical and logical person, and him being pretty amazing at reading people, they brought together a combination of skills that had served them well in case solving. The only thing that sometimes made her nervous about Tim was that at the end of each case, when all the solving was done, he always changed.

Day to day, he was pretty consistent in his nature. He was quite brilliant in what he did, and a real charmer. Ashley had learned early on in working with him that he could appear to not be focused on a situation while he was, in fact, taking in every tiny detail. In that, he was a bit of a master of disguise.

When she worked with him, she admired him for his work ethic and his skill base. She never looked at him with a romantic eye. He was handsome. He was also a player when it came to women. On each final day of every case they'd worked, he'd changed a little bit, implying he'd like to have a little bit more from her. She'd been surprised the first time it had happened. Now, she'd come to expect it.

Sitting in her car, she laughed softly to herself as she started the engine. Pondering her interactions with Tim would get her nowhere. She had a case to delve into and solve. Whenever that happened, everything else could wait.

CHAPTER 25

As he drove home to his apartment, Special Agent Tim Moore ran through his mind all that he had to do before he was picked up. He'd learned long ago to always have a small carry-on sized suitcase packed and ready to go, so that was already sorted. He ran through a checklist in his mind, double-checking that everything he'd need, he had already put in it. Satisfied that all he had to do was have a quick shower, put on clean clothes, and then grab his carry-on, his mind drifted elsewhere.

He and Ashley had worked on many cases, always with success. In his view, she was an incredible woman with an incredible mind. He knew he was good at his job, but she excelled in a completely different way of thinking from what he did. It had always kept him in awe of her. That she was an extremely beautiful woman was only a bonus.

More than once, he had mildly hinted to her that he'd like them to be more than just work colleagues. Those conversations never ended in his favor. He was glad they got on so well. Some might even call their relationship a friendship. That was nothing to be sad over. In some ways, he wished he could stop looking at her like he did, and just be happy with having her as a potential friend. That would, at least, stop all those uncomfortable speeches from happening.

As he pulled into his driveway, he grabbed his stuff and ran up to his apartment. Overall, he'd become pretty efficient in moving quickly when they were assigned a job. It felt like, in no time at all, he'd dumped his daily gear, showered, shaved, and applied the aftershave that he was pretty sure Ashley liked. All he had to do after that was gather up his previously packed carry-on. By the time Ashley turned up, he was happily standing at the curb, eagerly waiting to see her again.

"Ready to search for a missing woman?" Ashley said as Tim jumped into her car.

"Hell, yeah! Bring it on, I say," Tim replied, doing up his seatbelt. "It's odd, looking for someone just because of a favor, though, don't you think?"

Ashley looked at him and smiled.

"You and I have done a few cases now that weren't officially assigned cases," she said. "It only adds to the thrill, doesn't it!"

Tim laughed softly.

"Indeed, it does."

CHAPTER 26

After completing their long drive and checking in to their assigned motel, Ashley and Tim made their way to the police station.

"Do you think they even know we've been asked to work on this, given that it's a 'favor'?" Tim asked just before they entered the exterior doors of the building.

Ashley had considered the possibility that local law enforcement had no idea. She hoped that wasn't the case. Sometimes it felt unpleasant enough when they turned up and took over cases when they weren't really wanted. She didn't want to have to explain why they were there.

"Special Agents Power and Moore, I take it," they heard a male voice say as they entered, indirectly addressing Ashley's uncertainty about whether they were expected.

Turning to face the voice that had called out to them, both saw a man who appeared to be in his 40s. He wore no uniform at all. That produced uncertainty in both agents.

"Hello," Ashley said as she held out her hand. "I am Special Agent Ashley Power. And you are?"

"I'm the Chief. Don't be deterred by my appearance. It is only personal circumstance that has prevented me from being in uniform today," the man said as he shook Ashley's hand. "You can call me John. Everybody does," he continued as he unlocked a security door separating the public area from the work area beyond.

"You were informed of us coming to help in the missing woman case then?" Tim asked, reading the

Chief's body language during his question, and during the answer that was returned.

"Oh, yes. Come in here to my office and take a seat," John said. "Yes, the missing woman's family and her husband, Daniel Sloan, are all eager to find his wife. I trust you have read the details we sent through to the Bureau?"

"Yes," Ashley replied. "There wasn't a lot in the file we were presented with. Can you tell us any more about the case?"

The Chief sat back in his chair and looked at the two of them.

"I understand from what the husband has said that the young lady has been missing since last Friday. So far, he appears to be the last person to have seen her."

Ashley asked the obvious question.

"Do you think there's any chance he's involved?" she asked and watched as the Chief leaned forward, elbows resting on his desk.

"It's hard to say. It isn't inconceivable that the person who calls law enforcement is the one who committed a crime," the Chief said. "*He* didn't call us, of course…"

"He didn't?" Tim asked. That detail had been overlooked in the conveyance of information.

"No, Mrs. Sloan has two sisters she was due to meet with on Sunday. It was only when she didn't turn up that it was brought to our attention that she was missing."

Tim did the quick calculation in his head.

"Didn't you say she'd last been seen by her husband on Friday?" he asked. "Two whole days had passed? Why didn't he report her missing?"

John inhaled deeply before speaking.

"He has told our officer that the two of them had an intense argument on Friday morning. He had thought she would have gone to stay with her sisters or a friend to have time away from him."

"Convenient. Do you believe him?" Ashley asked.

John smiled at her.

"I have my reservations, but you are most welcome to conduct your investigation," he said. "People in this station are close to the family. It will be good to have some fresh eyes on the case. Sometimes people who aren't familiar with any of the people involved, see things that people close to it might not."

"We will certainly do our best, Chief," Ashley said. "For now, can you look at this file and confirm it has all that we need to get started?"

After receiving the printed file from her, John perused through it then handed it back.

"I believe it is all there," he said. "Is there anything else I can provide to help you?"

"No, thank you. We'll begin with interviewing the missing woman's friends and family straight away," Ashley replied as she stood and leaned forward to shake his hand. "We'll be in touch."

Outside the station, as they begin to climb into Ashley's car, Tim asked the obvious question.

"Where do we start?"

Once seated inside the car, Ashley replied.

"With the most obvious suspect - the husband."

CHAPTER 27

"Mr. Sloan, I'm Special Agent Power, and this is my colleague, Special Agent Moore. We're here to talk to you about your wife's disappearance," Ashley said when Daniel opened the door to his apartment.

"Yes, of course," Daniel replied. "Please come in."

"No work for you today, Mr. Sloan?" Tim asked. To some people, it might have sounded as if he were just curious. Ashley knew better. Tim never asked a question without having a reason for it. It was his way of understanding people. That skill was something that had helped in closing many cases they'd worked on together.

Daniel looked at him with a sober look on his face.

"No, of course not," he said. "My wife is missing. Work is the last thing on my mind."

"Can you tell us about the last time you saw Mrs. Sloan?" Ashley asked.

She watched as Daniel nodded, rubbed his hands together nervously, and began to speak.

"Friday morning was the last time I saw her. She left to go to work, and I haven't seen or heard from her since."

"And all was well between you?" Tim asked.

Daniel shook his head.

"No, we had an argument. It was all my fault. She'd been out with friends the night before, and I'd overreacted to seeing Flo hugging one of her male friends," he said, tears visibly beginning in his eyes. "I love her so much. It's been difficult for me to see her with other men. That is something I need to address. I do know that she didn't do anything wrong."

"Who was the man she was hugging?" Ashley asked.

"A long time friend. Grant is his first name. I think she's mentioned his last name. It might be Biddle or something like that, but I'm not sure," Daniel replied. "As far as I know, they've been friends for years. I don't think there was anything in it. When Flo and I were arguing, she pointed out that she'd hugged all of her friends that night. I just didn't see it."

Ashley nodded. She could sense Tim next to her, doing his thing in people analysis.

"We understand you didn't report her missing. Why not?" Tim asked.

Daniel looked visibly uncomfortable.

"When she walked out, she said she needed time away from me," he replied. "When she didn't come home that night, I assumed that was what she was doing. I thought she would have gone to see and stay with one of her sisters. They're close. It never occurred to me that she wasn't with either of them."

"Did you wonder if she'd gone to be with another man?" Ashley asked.

"No!" Daniel exclaimed passionately.

"But you were jealous. You said the entire argument of that morning was centered around her having just hugged another man, yet it didn't even cross your mind that she might have left you and gone to stay with another guy?" Tim pushed.

Upset, Daniel stood up and walked to the window.

"No, that didn't even feature in my thoughts," he said. "Friday night and all day Saturday, I thought she was taking some time just for herself. It wasn't until her sisters turned up here on Sunday afternoon that I even considered that something was more wrong than just us having an argument and her being upset with me."

"Did you call any of her friends or either of her sisters to check up on her?" Ashley asked, curious.

"No," Daniel replied as he shook his head. "I thought she needed space from me. If I'd called and tried to make contact with her, that wouldn't have helped." He paused as he returned to his seat. "Look, I can see that I've made a mess of everything. I shouldn't have been upset at Flo, I shouldn't have argued with her, and I should have been concerned when she didn't come home after work on Friday. None of those decisions that I made can be changed now. Please, can you find my wife?"

"That is why we are here, Mr. Sloan," Tim said. "Can you think of anyone who might want to hurt Mrs. Sloan? Or get back at you for something?"

"Flo and I do have a level of independence in our marriage, but as far as someone wanting to hurt her, no, I don't think so. She's a good person and a nice person. It seems unlikely she could upset anyone," Daniel replied.

"And you? Could there be someone who wants to hurt *you?*" Ashley asked.

Daniel took a few minutes to consider. He hadn't even pondered that Flo having left could have anything to do with someone wanting to hurt *him.*

"No, I don't think so," he replied. "I run my family business, but we don't have any enemies, as far as I know."

"You haven't received any messages or requests for money?"

"No," Daniel said, his thinking taking another turn. "You think she might have been ... kidnapped?"

"It's too early yet for us to come to that conclusion, but it is a possibility," Ashley answered quietly. "Your family is wealthy, I understand?"

"Yes, but I haven't received anything. If someone took Flo as a way to get money, they would have contacted me by now, wouldn't they?"

"Or your parents," Tim said. "Could it be that they might have received some kind of ransom demand?"

"No," Daniel replied as he shook his head. "I can't

imagine my parents would keep something like that from me, and if there *was* a ransom demand, they would have paid it, and Flo would be home now!"

Tim watched Daniel's face. The thing that stood out most to him was that Daniel Sloan was someone who knew how to wear a mask, and wear it well. That made things more difficult in reading him. He seemed the type of person who could present innocence with perfection, all the while being completely guilty of wrongdoing.

"I think that is all we need for now," Tim said, standing up. "Can you give us your parents' address? We would like to talk to them also."

Ashley followed Tim's lead and stood. She'd long ago learned that when he initiated action, it was wise to go along with it.

"Thank you, Mr. Sloan…" Ashley started to say as she held out her hand to Daniel.

"Please find my wife. Please bring her home to me."

"We will do our best," Ashley reassured him. "Here's my card. Please call me if you hear from her, or if you think of anything else that might assist us in our investigation."

Tim watched as Daniel took the business card and escorted them out of the front door.

Nothing was said between the two agents until they were back in the car and a fair distance away from the apartment complex.

"What do you think?" Ashley asked. "Is he a possible suspect, or a *likely* suspect?"

Tim looked at her, his face serious.

"I think he could be either, or neither. Mr. Sloan is almost impossible to read."

"Even for you?" Ashley asked, surprised. "I've never heard you say that about anyone."

"I know, but in his case, I do think that he could be the reason for his wife's disappearance, but he equally might have nothing to do with it," Tim said. "I think that once we talk to everyone else *about* Daniel Sloan, we'll have a better understanding of who he is, and what part he might have played in this."

"Alright," Ashley said. "Let's go and see his parents first. I think Flo's family and friends will have a different view to offer, but I'm curious to see what his mother and father can tell us."

CHAPTER 28

"Mr. and Mrs. Sloan, we are here to discuss the disappearance of your daughter-in-law," Tim said when they were shown into the Sloan household and greeted by Daniel's parents.

"Disappearance? I don't understand," Daniel's father said.

Tim looked at both parents in surprise. Each of them appeared to have a genuine look of shock on their faces.

"You didn't know that Flo Sloan is missing?" he asked them.

In response, they both shook their heads.

"No! I … we … no, we haven't spoken to Daniel for several days," Daniel's mother said as she looked at his father. "Well, *I* haven't. Have you?"

Once again, Daniel's father shook his head.

"No," he replied as he turned to look at each of the agents seated on the sofa facing him. "We don't see Daniel and Flo very often these days. I thought they might come and see us after their honeymoon and tell us all about Paris, but they haven't made contact since they got back. As is usually the case with children when they grow and start their own lives, Daniel is very busy and active in his work at our company. We have him and Flo over for dinner now and then, but it has been quite a while since they last visited."

"I know this may seem an impertinent question, but is their relationship happy, in your opinion?" Ashley asked.

It was Daniel's mother who answered immediately.

"Oh, yes!" she exclaimed. "Flo is a joy to have as a

new addition to our family. We all love her."

"Yes, Mrs. Sloan," Tim began. "But do you think they, as a couple, are genuinely *happy?*"

He watched Daniel's father as he pushed the question. Mr. Sloan's facial response was less guarded than that of his wife. Tim and Ashley waited, giving both parents time to truly consider the question.

"There have been times when they have seemed tense together," Daniel's father finally answered. "He has never said that they are unhappy, however. Why do you ask this anyway? Shouldn't you be looking for Flo if she is missing, like you say she is?"

Ashley watched the couple. She hadn't grown up as part of a wealthy family. It had taken time for her to hone her skills in looking past the façade of wealth when visiting anyone involved in a case, and seeing them just as normal human beings. She had to admit, Mr. and Mrs. Sloan seemed to be a secure couple. Unknown was how real the façade currently being presented was. She looked briefly at Tim. He would have a better understanding of that.

"We are here as part of our investigation, Mr. Sloan," Tim replied. "Can you tell us if you have received any kind of request for money?"

Daniel's father looked horrified.

"If we'd received that, then we would have known our daughter-in-law was missing!" he exclaimed. "No, no kind of demand has come to us." He paused, considering. "Do you think it will? You think someone has taken Flo to bribe us into paying money to get her back?"

Tim found the use of the word 'bribe' interesting but didn't point it out. Instead, he nodded.

"We do think it is possible, given your family's social and financial status, that Flo might have been abducted as a way to get money through ransom."

Ashley saw Daniel's mother place her hand on her

husband's arm. The movement delivered a clear vision of distress. How real it was, was difficult to gauge.

"Were you happy when Daniel told you he wanted to marry someone who I understand was not as financially well off as your family is, Mr. Sloan?"

On hearing the question, Daniel's father stood up abruptly.

"What a thing to ask! My son always wanted to find someone he could respect, who he felt wouldn't want him just for his money. In Flo, I truly believe that he found that," he said sternly. "Would I have chosen her for him? No, not if we lived a century ago and marriage was about transactions! But we do not live like that now, and although I may not show love much in traditional ways, I do love my son. All I've ever wanted was his happiness. When he brought Flo home to meet us, it was clear to see how they felt about one another. Any parent who can't be happy to see such a thing on their child's face should not be a parent at all!"

"Darling, please sit down," Mrs. Sloan said as she guided her husband back onto the sofa they shared. After he was seated, she faced the agents. "Our son loves Flo. Do they have problems? Yes, I am sure they do. That is a part of being married. Sometimes, it takes hard work and compromise. Sometimes, one partner is left feeling much happier than the other. That doesn't mean that a husband and wife don't care for each other."

"No, of course not," Ashley said as she stood up. "Well, thank you for your time. We will leave you now."

"What will you do?" Daniel's father asked, prompting Tim and Ashley to both turn and face the couple again. "What will you do to find my son's wife?"

"We have interviews to conduct, Mr. Sloan," Tim replied. "Your daughter-in-law has close friends and family. We are hopeful someone will know what has happened to her, and where she is."

"Please bring her back. She makes our Daniel so

happy," Mrs. Sloan said.

Tim and Ashley nodded and excused themselves.

"Well, that was interesting," Ashley said as they climbed into the car once again.

"Yes. They did seem surprised by the news that Flo was missing," Tim replied. "Am I the only one who finds it odd that Daniel didn't tell them? I mean, if I had a wife and she went missing, I'd reach out to everyone, even if just to ask them if they'd seen her."

"Yes, I can't figure out why he wouldn't have told them, or called them to check if they'd seen her or heard from her," Ashley agreed before pausing, thoughtful. "And not only that, but when we told Daniel that we wanted to speak to his parents, he didn't point out that he hadn't told them Flo was missing. There didn't even seem to be any hindsight there that prompted him to think he *should* call his parents and tell them about his wife's disappearance."

"I agree. It does seem like there's a complete disconnect between him saying they hadn't received any ransom demand, and them saying that they didn't even know that she was missing," Tim said.

"What does that mean, though? It is possible that he's just all mixed up in his mind right now, as anyone would be if their loved one disappeared," Ashley pondered out loud.

"Yes, I imagine it would be a confusing time for him, and for everyone who knows her," Tim agreed. "I'm getting peckish. Do you think we can grab something to eat before we visit anyone else?"

Ashley smiled at him. Good old Tim. Some things were always the same with him. It was that kind of reliability that kept Ashley feeling comfortable with slowly building a friendship with him, in addition to their work relationship.

"We can. I want to call each of Flo's sisters anyway, so I'll do that while you're ordering," Ashley answered.

"That looks like a small mall up there. What do you feel like?"

"Food is food to me," Tim replied as he grinned at her. "You know that."

Ashley chuckled softly and nodded. Nothing more needed to be said.

CHAPTER 29

Driving up the driveway to the house of Flo's oldest sister, Kim, Ashley was surprised.

"Wow, that is more of a house than I expected."

Tim looked at her. "Why?"

Ashley shrugged her shoulders.

"I don't know," she said. "From what I've read about Flo, she seems to be a down to earth woman who isn't from a wealthy family. I guess I expected her sister would be the same - modest financially, I mean."

"Well, we don't know anything about Kim yet. Let's go and suss her out!" Tim said eagerly.

His fervor made Ashley smile. Tim was always enthusiastic, but after eating a meal, his enthusiasm seemed to grow to new heights.

They climbed out of the car and walked up to the front door. After knocking, the door was opened within only seconds.

"Oh, thank you for coming," Kim said, holding out her hands to take Ashley's in hers, then Tim's. "Please come in and sit down."

Once seated, it was Kim who began the questioning.

"Have you found anything out about my sister yet?" she asked, obviously full of concern. "Please tell me you have something."

Ashley shook her head. "Sorry, Mrs...."

"Oh, please call me Kim. Everybody does."

"Kim," Ashley responded as she nodded. "We have only spoken to three people so far. We understand that you were the person who made the initial call, reporting your sister's disappearance?"

"Yes," Kim replied with a look of disgust on her face. "Daniel hadn't even reported her missing! When he said that he'd last seen her on Friday, and it was then Sunday, I didn't know what to think."

"How do you see the marriage between your sister and Mr. Sloan?" Tim asked.

"Oh, they've been together for a couple of years, but they are only newlyweds, so marriage is something they still seem to be adjusting to. I think that it has been rocky at times," Kim said slowly. "I do believe Flo does love Daniel, but more than once, she's spoken of times when he's acted a bit over the top."

"Over the top, how?" Ashley asked.

Kim took a moment to assemble her reply.

"Flo said that there have been times when she's interacted with one man or another, and Daniel has acted as though he thinks she might be having an affair with the guy," she said. "It's so crazy. I don't know how she deals with it."

"Do you think there *is* any chance that your sister's having an affair?" Tim dared to ask.

"No!' Kim exclaimed without hesitation. "They might have had the odd issue, but no. There is no way that Flo would do that to anybody, let alone her husband! And besides, she does love him. I am sure of that."

"Can you tell us who the men were that Daniel got jealous over?" Ashley asked, already knowing that Daniel had mentioned Grant.

"She mentioned a couple of incidents that happened when they were on their honeymoon in Paris. Flo said she saw an old work colleague or teacher or something like that - someone she hadn't seen for years anyway. Daniel lost it over that, and then again over her speaking to a male waiter or bartender. I don't know the exact details. Some things she's told me, and some things I heard from one of her friends when I called them on

Sunday.

"I think there's also been an ongoing issue with Flo having two good friends who are male. From what she's said, I got the impression that Daniel wasn't too impressed with that either," she said before shrugging her shoulders. "It's always seemed like he just doesn't like her talking to any man. I don't get why he would be so worried. I mean, he's a good-looking man, so he can't have any lack of confidence."

Tim watched Kim's face as she delivered her lengthy dialogue. Something he never tired of was watching people.

"Do you think it's because of a lack of confidence, or a need to control?" he asked.

"I … I never thought about it like that," Kim said, surprised. "I can only speculate from what she tells me, but it seems like he's generally pretty good about her making up her own mind in things. She said when they had the kids-or-no-kids talk, he said he wanted kids, and soon. When she told him she wanted to wait, she said he accepted it easily enough," she said before pausing to consider Tim's question further. "Hmm, I don't know about that one. Maybe it *is* a control thing. I don't know if she knows why he is like he is. She's never said as much to me."

"What do you think might have happened to your sister, Kim?" Ashley asked. "Where do *you* think she could be?"

Presented with the questions, Kim began to weep.

"I don't know," she said. "It isn't like her to not contact me or Amber. On Sunday, when we were all supposed to meet for brunch, I'm sure she would have called to cancel if that was all that was going on. She's never missed a brunch, and she's never not turned up when she was expected somewhere. One thing I know about my sister is that she's reliable and she's punctual. I can't imagine she'd let anyone down."

"What about other aspects of her life? What else is she involved in?" Ashley asked.

"She works on big projects for the newspaper," Kim replied. "I know some of those have been serious. She's called some big companies out on their behaviors, I think, but with those, she always asked that her name not be put on the article."

Tim found the statement perplexing.

"A newspaper journalist who doesn't want their name associated with an article they've written?" he asked. "I can't say I've ever heard of that."

"Well, Flo was different that way," Kim said. "She regarded herself as a writer, not a journalist, even though she did the investigating and reporting. For her, it was the love of putting words together that truly inspired her. I mean, she seemed glad when finishing an investigation and report, but she'd be happy about the *way* she'd written something, rather than *what* she'd written, if that makes sense."

"I can understand that," Ashley said, nodding. "Is there any particular article that she's written lately, which had her worried if it got out that she was the one behind it, do you know?"

Kim shook her head.

"No, she never gives me specific details," she said. "Her boss should be able to help you with that, though, shouldn't she? All I know is that sometimes Flo is very excited about what she's working on. At other times, she has given the impression that she was working on something that could hurt one big corporation or other," she said and paused. "Sorry, I can't offer you anything more specific. We meet up every weekend for a catch-up, but Flo does have a way of casting conversation away from her so that she can listen rather than talk. I sometimes ask her if she's happy in her marriage…"

"And is she? In your opinion?" Tim asked.

"For the most part, I think she is. Daniel puts her

through the wringer sometimes with his possessiveness, but my sister is a strong woman. Certainly, she has seemed to bloom in that since she's known him."

"What do you mean?" Ashley asked.

"Well, I think the first time she saw his jealous streak, she was a bit intimidated by it and just wanted to soothe him," Kim said. "Over time, as there've been more and more occurrences with him acting weird when she's around guys, I think she's developed skills in standing up to him. The last time she mentioned it, she said if he acted that way again, she was going to tell him straight to do whatever he had to in order to fix his paranoia."

"And did he? Do anything to fix it?"

Kim shrugged her shoulders.

"I don't know," she replied. "She told me that when we last met up. That was Sunday before last."

"Did she say what she would do if he *didn't* fix his paranoia?" Tim asked.

"No," Kim said, shaking her head.

"Was that the last time the two of you spoke?" Tim asked.

"Yes," Kim replied. "The three of us prefer to meet up in person once a week and have a good catch up then. Life gets so busy during the week. We have a set time and place we meet for brunch, so we don't tend to contact each other at all any other time."

"Okay," Tim said, nodding. "Is there anyone you can think of who might want to hurt your sister?"

Kim looked horrified.

"No! Oh my god, do you think someone's *hurt* her?"

Tim could see that Kim hadn't even considered the obvious possibility.

"We don't know," he said. "Is there anything else you can think of that might give us some direction in where to look in regard to her disappearance? Can you think of anyone else that we should talk to? Anyone who might have been upset at her, or upset that she married Daniel perhaps?"

"Oh, umm, no, I don't think so," Kim replied. "I mean, Daniel is well off, you know. I don't know anything about his past with other women. I guess someone from his past *might* have been upset about him getting married? He was a sought-after bachelor for so long, after all. I'm really not the one to ask about that, though. All I can say is that Flo has never mentioned any of Daniel's ex-girlfriends to me. I don't know if she knows about them or not."

"And people from *her* past, who she has been involved with?" Ashley asked. "Is there anyone there that might have been upset by her getting married?"

"Brent is the only guy she's had a serious relationship with, that I know of. They were together for a couple of years, but I think he cheated on her so she walked out on him, if I remember correctly. She hasn't mentioned him for a long time, though. If she's had anything to do with him since she met Daniel, she hasn't said so to me," Kim replied. "Where is my sister?" she asked all of a sudden, tears beginning.

"We will find her," Ashley said quietly. "If there is anything else you can remember that you think might be helpful, please call me."

Kim accepted the business card that was handed to her.

"Thank you," she said as she wiped her eyes. "Have you spoken to him? Daniel?" she asked, looking at each agent.

Tim nodded. "We have."

"Do you think he has something to do with this? Do you think he's done something to her?"

"Do *you?*" Ashley asked, taking note of the look of concern on Kim's face.

"I was mad at him when I found out he hadn't seen her for two nights, but he hadn't thought to tell anyone, even the cops," said Kim. "He is supposed to love my sister. I still don't get why he didn't tell anyone."

"Well, we will follow up all possibilities, but please do call if you think of anything, or if you hear from her," Ashley said.

"One more question, Kim," Tim asked. "Forgive me, but I can't help but notice your home. Can I ask what you do for a living that enables you to be able to afford somewhere like this?"

"I'm a surgeon," Kim replied, smiling sadly. "I only work part-time at the local hospital. It does pay well, but my husband is a neurosurgeon, so he is the one who brings in the big bucks."

"Do you or your husband have any disgruntled patients that you can think of?" Tim asked. "Or do you know of anything that has happened that might make a patient, or a family member of theirs, want to hurt you or your husband?"

Kim's face revealed the surprise she felt upon hearing the question.

"You think someone might have taken my sister as a way to get back at *me* for something?"

"We have to look at all possibilities," Tim replied. "Have you received anything threatening that you can think of? Even if it's something you think is unrelated, it would be good for us to follow up as part of our investigation."

"No," Kim said. "I mean, in surgery, things do happen. Sometimes we lose a patient. That is part of the job and it always ends in distress for families, but nobody has done anything or said anything that felt like a threat."

"Okay, well, thank you," Ashley said as they neared the front door. "We'll be in touch."

"Do you think that's a possibility?" Ashley asked Tim when they were driving away. "The sister or her husband having an enemy somewhere, who is using Flo as some kind of payback?"

"I don't know. My gut says no, but *someone* knows where Flo is," Tim replied.

"Do they?" asked Ashley. "For all we know, she has just taken off for some time out, as Daniel suggested."

"Yeah, I don't like that theory at all," Tim said, scoffing. "Maybe if it was just Daniel who she'd shunned temporarily, but unless Kim is lying, it sounds like Flo would normally be reliable in seeing her and the other sister. That part of it makes me think that wherever Flo is, she isn't there by choice."

"Okay, well, it's probably too late to talk to anyone else today. Let's go back to the motel," Ashley said. "A good night's sleep might help us to consider new possibilities to explore tomorrow."

As they walked into the lobby of their motel, Tim turned to her.

"I'll contact tech and get them to check Flo's phone and bank account activity," he said. "Maybe that'll show up something that can at least tell us if she's still alive."

Ashley nodded. "Good idea. I'll contact each of these four friends and find out when and where we can talk to them tomorrow. Meet up for breakfast?"

Tim grinned his brilliant not-thinking-about-work grin.

"Yep! Usual time of six-thirty?"

"Sounds good," Ashley said as the elevator doors opened on her floor. "Sleep well!"

"You too," Tim replied just before the doors closed again. As soon as he was alone in the elevator, he felt just that - alone. It was a feeling he was used to but never liked. He was also aware that the times that the feeling was strongest, were always just after he'd spent a decent amount of time with Ashley.

CHAPTER 30

"Hello," Christine said as she greeted the two agents who had just introduced themselves to her. They'd met up at a local café during Christine's lunch break. "You said on the phone that Flo still hasn't gone home?"

"As far as we know, that is the case, yes," Ashley said, sitting down. "You still haven't heard from her?"

"No," Christine replied, shaking her head. "We don't usually chat too much on the phone anyway, but I have been calling her phone and trying to leave a message."

"Trying?" Tim asked.

"Yes, I was able to leave one on Sunday just after Kim called me to ask if I'd seen Flo. Since then, it keeps saying that the voicemail box is at maximum capacity, and no more messages can be left," she replied. "I guess a lot of people have left messages for her, and she isn't deleting them."

Ashley watched Christine's face as she talked. It didn't give much away.

"Do you think something has happened to her?" Christine asked. "Something … bad?"

"We aren't ready to accept that quite yet. We still have to follow up a few things."

"I only saw her last Thursday," Christine said, sounding distracted.

"Did she mention anything that she was worried about? Is there anyone you can think of that she was having problems with?" Tim asked.

Christine shook her head again.

"She didn't mention anyone. I mean, she had the

usual things to say about Daniel, but whenever she mentions him in a negative light, she then plumps him up in a positive one. I think it's just their way to have a little bit of a roller coaster thing going on."

"Can you elaborate?" Ashley asked.

"Oh, just that they generally do seem happy together but, now and then, Flo would say Daniel was acting a little odd. Mostly, I think it was to do with Toby or Grant. Daniel came with Flo to our monthly catch ups a few times. When he was with us, he seemed nice enough, although he did look at the guys a bit funnily sometimes. I don't think he particularly liked her having friends who were guys," Christine replied. "It was a bit strange really. I think the very reason Flo brought him along on those nights was to show him that we *all* are just friends. There's never been any crossover there romantically. We get on well, and we've known each other forever."

"Has Flo ever mentioned any other aspect of their relationship that might have been difficult for her?" Tim asked.

"Not that I can remember," said Christine. "Like I said, generally I think that she is happy. It's just now and then that the jealousy thing revs up a bit. She's always seemed able to handle it pretty well, though. I don't think I could put up with a partner being jealous over every single man I spoke to. I mean, I work with about forty of them. That would drive a partner like Daniel nutty!"

Tim had listened carefully to what was being said. The last sentence was one that would stick in his mind, he was sure. He and Ashley had worked plenty of cases where it had turned out to be a jealous partner who had killed out of rage, having almost lost their mind. Tim hoped this case would turn out differently. He wasn't ready to accept the missing woman as dead yet.

"And there's nothing that you can think of that might have happened to her? There haven't been any people or situations that could have been dangerous, that you know of?" Ashley asked.

"Well, her work sometimes gets a bit hairy. I know she was working on something to do with a large company leaching chemicals into the ground. She wasn't able to talk about that at the time, but the article was in the paper, so I'm guessing it's not confidential anymore," Christine said. "I think the newspaper might have gotten into a bit of trouble over that one. The company in question tried to say the newspaper had made everything up, but that isn't likely with Flo being the one who investigated it all."

"She wouldn't lie or stretch the truth?" Tim asked.

"No, I don't think so," Christine replied. "Her job is too important to her. I think she's had a few job assignments like that one, though. Maybe one of them isn't too happy with her…"

Tim and Ashley listened, asked a few more questions, and then left. From Christine, they had learned a few more small snippets of information, but it had started to feel like no matter who they questioned, the same answers always came back at them. Flo had worked on assignments that could have been damaging for large companies. Flo had an obsessively jealous husband.

As they left, both agents felt frustrated.

"There has to be new information out there somewhere," Ashley said as they climbed into her car.

"I agree," Tim said, nodding. "It's getting a bit repetitive with everyone saying the same things."

"Well, let's move on to the next friend. Grant is the one Daniel said he had the argument with Flo about. Surely he must be able to shed some light on something new," Ashley said.

"Either that or he's going to show us that there *was* something to their hug, and he's involved," Tim said, ending the conversation.

CHAPTER 31

Grant looked at the two agents that sat across from him in the local library.

"Is she really missing?" he asked them, his face grave.

Tim nodded as he studied Grant closely.

"It appears so," he replied. "When did you last see Mrs. Sloan?"

"Thursday last week. There's a group of five of us who meet up once a month for dinner. Flo was there, and left when we all did," Grant replied.

"Did she seem in any way upset or different than usual? Was there anything that she mentioned that might have played a part in her disappearance?" Ashley asked. She suspected that all four friends might end up saying the same thing, but she still had to ask every one of them.

"No, not really," Grant said and paused. "She mentioned some weird instances with Daniel in Paris. It was something about how she'd spoken to a few different men in passing, and he'd gone psycho over it."

"Psycho?" Tim asked for clarification.

"Oh, sorry, maybe not that far. She indicated that he'd been pretty upset by her chatting to other guys. I think even the restaurant staff got pulled into it, from what she said. It seems to have been a constant thing throughout their marriage so far, to be honest. Why she puts up with him, I have no idea," Grant replied.

"You've met him?"

"Yep, we got to see him at the wedding, of course,

and Flo also brought him along to a few of our catch-up nights too," Grant replied.

"How did you feel about him being there on those nights?" Ashley asked.

"It was a bit strange," Grant admitted as he shrugged his shoulders. "As a general rule, none of us bring partners on those nights - not even Stacey, who's in a long-term relationship. It's usually just the five of us catching up as old friends, so I've never thought it could be much fun for a partner, especially when we start reminiscing about memories that only we can relate to," he said and paused for a moment. "But I mean, apart from the way he looked at me and Toby, Daniel did seem as if he *wanted* to relax and fit in. I do think he tried, which Flo seemed to appreciate."

"You said he looked at you and Toby … differently from the others, do you mean?"

"Yeah, I probably can't explain it very well. I feel like every time I've come face to face with Daniel, it's like looking into the face of someone who is a competitor. It's almost like he's challenging me at something, even though he never uses words to say that," Grant replied. "But I hardly know him. My perception could be completely off."

Tim watched and assessed Grant's demeanor.

"How did you feel about Flo?" he asked.

"She's one of my closest friends," Grant replied.

"You don't have any other feelings for her?" Ashley asked. "Romantic ones?"

"No!" Grant exclaimed, surprised. "We've all grown up together. It wouldn't be normal to look at Flo or Christine or Stacey in that kind of way."

"No lines have been crossed within your group?"

"If you're asking if any of us have slept with each other, then no, not as far as I know anyway. I can only speak for myself and tell you that *I* haven't gone there with any of the girls. That would just be … weird,"

Grant said. "I haven't seen Daniel at all since I got the news about Flo. Is he ... is he a suspect in Flo's disappearance?"

"Do you think he should be?" Ashley asked, studying his face.

"All I can offer is my perspective, and that's only based on what Flo's told me," Grant replied.

"And what is your perspective?" Tim asked.

"From what she's said, they do have their moments of destructive behavior, driven mainly, I think, by his jealousy issues. But overall, Flo does generally sound happy with her relationship and marriage to him."

"Do you think Daniel would have it in him to hurt someone?" Ashley asked.

Grant looked at her, shocked.

"You think she's hurt?" he asked. "No, that can't be. Surely she's just taking some time out."

"Would that be normal behavior for her?"

"No," Grant answered, shaking his head. "I can't remember her ever saying that she's done that, but then we only catch up every few weeks these days. There possibly is a lot more that goes on during the times when we don't speak."

Tim listened and watched. His gut told him that the man before him was being honest and had nothing to hide.

"One more question," Ashley said. "Do you know how Flo goes to work?"

Grant considered then shook his head.

"I have no idea."

"Does she drive a car?"

"I'm guessing so," Grant said. "I mean, she definitely *used* to, but when she comes to our catch up nights, she always seems to be walking. I think they live not too far from the restaurant."

Tim nodded.

"You *think?*" Tim asked. "You don't go there? To her

home, I mean."

"No, I've never been to their place, and Flo's never invited me. She never talked about the possibility, but I suspect that Daniel might not like us there anyway," Grant said. "In saying that, though, as a group, we never go to each other's homes these days. It's just easier for everyone to meet up at one set time each month, in one set location."

Ashley and Tim looked at each other. It was slow going, trying to find any information that seemed useful to the case, but they still had more interviews to conduct yet.

"Is there anything you can think of that might help us to further search for Flo, Grant?" Ashley asked. "Even the smallest of things can be a clue."

"No," Grant replied. "To be honest, if I hadn't heard from you guys or Flo's sister, I don't think I would even know Flo was missing right now. I haven't heard from Daniel at all, so I'm guessing he didn't think her friends would be interested in knowing that. Either that or he didn't think we were worthy or something."

"That's an odd thing to say," Tim said quietly. "Worthy?"

"I just mean ... well, Daniel seems a bit more ... I don't know ... upper class, I guess. I have often wondered if maybe that's why he didn't like Flo spending time with us. Maybe he thinks we're below him."

"Interesting," Tim said. "Do you think your friends think that too?"

"I have no idea," Grant replied shrugging his shoulders. "That's just my perception, and I've never said that to anyone. It might not be in any way true or real. It's just something I've wondered from time to time, given the way he always looked at me."

"Okay," said Tim, nodding. "Well, I think we've taken up enough of your time."

"Yeah, I do need to get back to work," Grant replied

as he stood up. "Please find her. I know I only see her once a month, but I do consider her one of my best friends. If she has just gone away for some time out, that really would be out of character, I think. Even if she didn't contact me or the others to say she was leaving, I can't see her not letting at least one of her sisters know. They're close," he said quietly. "I just … I just can't see Flo leaving and not telling someone."

"Thank you," Ashley said. "You have been helpful. Please call us if you think of anything more that might be of assistance to us."

"Sure," Grant replied.

As Tim and Ashley walked away, both were quiet. Once back in Ashley's car, they looked at one another.

"General consensus seems to be that Flo isn't the kind of person who would likely leave town and not say a word to anyone about it," Ashley said.

"Yeah, it does seem that way, doesn't it," Tim agreed. "We still have to talk to the other two friends, but I'm thinking it's time we went to her workplace and had a chat with her boss. What do you think?"

"Yes, that could provide something different for us to consider. A few people now have mentioned she works on cases that could upset some big companies," Ashley replied as she started the engine. "Let's go there now. The sister said they went to the premises on Sunday and it was closed, so I'm guessing it probably is open during regular office hours."

CHAPTER 32

"Hello, Ms. Canon. I am Special Agent Power, and this is Special Agent Moore," Ashley said when they'd been escorted into the large office of the local newspaper's CEO.

"Yes, I was alerted to your coming. How can I help you?" Suzy Canon asked as she indicated to the agents to sit down.

Tim looked at Ashley in surprise. The CEO didn't even look as though she had a staff member missing.

"We are here to talk about Fiona Sloan - Flo," Tim said. "Is it possible to find out when she was last on the premises?"

"Of course," Suzy replied, nodding. "We have the best security cameras here, so I can ask our security team to check that for you, but what is this about?"

"Mrs. Sloan hasn't been heard from or seen by her husband or sisters since last week, which appears to go against her nature," Ashley said. "Do you not work with her?"

"I assign her jobs to do," Suzy confirmed, confusion evident on her face. "Last week - Friday - she had a deadline for an article she'd been working on. The article was published, so I know that she *did* submit it. Whether she did it here in person, I cannot say."

"When did you last see her, Ms. Canon?" Tim asked.

Suzy looked thoughtful for a minute or two before she spoke.

"I was away all of last week at a conference, so it must be ... Wednesday before last? We had our usual meeting that day, where she tells me how her current assignment is going."

"Wednesday, two weeks ago," Tim said quietly. "Did she seem normal in that meeting? Nothing seemed off about her?"

"No, not that I noticed," Suzy replied. "She was confident that she was going to meet the deadline last Friday, and I had no doubt she would. Flo is one of the hardest working journalists we have."

"What about any articles she may have written that could have caused upset with anyone?" Ashley asked.

"Yes, well, that is another story," Suzy responded. "A while back, Flo investigated and reported on a company - HD Prosthetics. The body of the report shared details of how they've been letting chemicals leach into the grounds around their plant."

"And you think this could have caused upset?" Tim asked.

"Not could have ... *did!* They came at us with a lawsuit. It wasn't an easy time, let me tell you," Suzy replied. "For that report, Flo asked that her name be left off the article, so it was. It isn't usual practice around here for other writers, but I think she quite likes a bit of anonymity."

"Why do you think that is, Ms. Canon?" Tim asked.

Suzy looked directly at him, taking her time before she answered.

"Flo always said that what she wanted to do was write, not report," she said. "It took me a while to understand what she meant when she said that. I think with her, it was more the formation of words in print than what those words actually said, if that makes sense. It wasn't about the message being delivered. It was about how she could best *write* it."

"Can I ask, if she was due to hand in her assignment last Friday, would you not have expected her to be at work these past couple of days?" Tim asked.

"No, Flo enjoys having flexibility in her work, and I know that she clocks up the hours, so I'm glad to let her have it. It is quite normal for her to take a day or two off after she finishes an assignment," Suzy said. "She once described it to me as her way of cleansing her mind before starting on the next job. She's always done it, so I haven't been assuming anything is wrong."

"What is it?" Tim asked, noticing her face change.

"Did you say she's been missing since last week?" Suzy asked. In response to Ashley and Tim both nodding, she continued. "I don't understand why her husband didn't call if that is the case. Am I missing something?"

Ashley kept asking the same question over and over in her mind. No matter who she and Tim spoke to, the conversation kept returning to the fact that Daniel Sloan hadn't told anyone that his wife hadn't been seen in a couple of days.

"Let me call security now, while you're here. I'm sure they'll be able to provide footage from our security cameras," Suzy continued as she picked up the phone. A few minutes later, files were sent through to her computer. "I have footage here. Do you want to watch it now, or would you like me to put it on a USB drive for you to take away?"

"Both, please," Tim said, standing and walking around to Suzy's side of the desk. "Can you show us Friday's footage?"

"Yes," Suzy replied and opened the first file. "Shall I play it at the highest speed?"

"Yes, I just want to see if Flo can be seen entering or leaving on Friday."

It took a surprisingly short time to look through the footage and find what they were looking for. Even with it showing at the speed it was, there was enough clarity to identify people coming and going.

"So, Flo arrived at work just before seven-thirty in

the morning, then left just after ten. Two and a half hours she spent here," Tim said to Ashley, who was still sitting on the other side of the desk, thinking.

"Was that normal?" Ashley asked Suzy. "For her to come in for only a couple of hours and then leave?"

"Yes," Suzy confirmed. "Like I said, she was trustworthy in making up hours, so she had the freedom to come and go as she needed to, so long as the work was done and her required hours were met each fortnight."

"Alright. If we can get that footage on a USB drive, that would be appreciated," Tim said. Almost instantly, Suzy handed it to him. "Can you also tell us, do you know how Flo came to work each day?"

"Oh, I don't know about every single day, but I have seen her arriving quite often in her car. I don't know what kind of car it is, only that it's a small red hatchback."

Ashley's attention was captured. So far, nobody had mentioned Flo owning such a car.

"And you've seen her in that recently?"

"She was driving it the last time I saw her," Suzy confirmed, nodding. "I remember because we laughed when we both got out of our cars at the same time and immediately saw that we'd both picked up sweet treats for our meeting."

"And that was Wednesday before last? You're sure that you saw her that day, and she had driven to work in her car - a red hatchback?"

"Yes, I am one hundred percent sure," Suzy said before leaning forward. "Has something seriously happened to Flo? This isn't just her taking a couple of days off work then?"

"We don't believe so," Ashley replied. "She hasn't been seen by anyone and she hasn't been answering her phone or responding to voicemail messages left for her. As far as we can tell, the last place she was seen was here in this office building on Friday."

Tim moved around the desk to join Ashley before he turned back to face Suzy once more.

"Thank you for your help, Ms. Canon. We'll review this footage further, but if you think of anything that might be useful to us, please call," he said as he handed her his card.

"Yes, of course," Suzy said, her face finally showing concern for the wellbeing of her employee. "Can you please let me know what you find? It doesn't seem I will hear anything from Flo's other half."

"We will," Ashley replied. "Thank you."

As they walked out of the large office building, Tim made his usual request of any day.

"Shall we find somewhere to get lunch and go over what we're thinking so far?"

Ashley smiled at him. Her mind was busy, assessing all that they'd been told, but when it was just the two of them, she couldn't help but enjoy the grin that only Tim could deliver.

"Absolutely!" she replied, making him smile even more.

CHAPTER 33

"So!" Tim said as the two of them settled at a table in a steakhouse he'd located. Before he could say anything more, a waitress came up to them. It wasn't missed by Ashley that the waitress instantly gave Tim the kind of smile that he so often received from women. It was something Ashley was well used to but never tired of seeing.

"What can I get you, handsome?" the waitress asked Tim directly, not making eye contact with Ashley at all.

"Oh, thank you for being so prompt," Tim responded. "Can we please have a few more minutes, though? We haven't looked at menus yet."

The waitress laughed softly as she blushed.

"Oh, yes, sorry. Of course you haven't. Here they are," she said as she handed two menus into Tim's hands. "I'll come back in a few minutes."

"Thank you," Tim said, already noticing the look on Ashley's face. "What?" he asked her when the waitress had walked away.

"What indeed, Timothy!" Ashley said, grinning at him as she teased him.

His response - as always - was only to laugh out loud. He was fairly constant in attracting attention from women. It was something that often proved handy, especially when working on cases. While some women would close down when it came to talking to Ashley, they opened in full bloom when Tim looked at them, even if he asked the same question Ashley just had.

"Hmm, now what looks good?" Tim asked as he

opened his menu, smiling but not looking at his partner as he did so.

"Well, I'm thinking that the waitress thinks *you* do," Ashley said, making Tim laugh again.

"Now, now, Ms. Power. We are here to eat, so look at your menu and stop giving me a hard time," he responded.

Twenty minutes later, conversation was underway while both agents indulged in their meals.

"There's one thing that I just can't get past," Tim said. "Why didn't Daniel Sloan report his wife missing? He said that she'd said she wanted time away from him, but he didn't say that she did anything that would indicate she was going away for a length of time. I mean, he didn't say that she packed a bag or booked tickets to go anywhere, so I'm guessing that those things never happened."

"Or he just didn't mention it," Ashley added.

"Maybe," Tim said. "We need to question him again. We need to find out if Flo *did* pack anything to take with her because, let's face it, even if you go away overnight, you still take a few vital things like your toothbrush, right?"

"Usually, unless she made a last-minute decision to leave and the idea of keeping her teeth clean just wasn't something she considered important," Ashley said.

"Yeah, I guess. If she decided to leave in a hurry, she might have thought it best to go without going home to grab anything, especially if she thought Daniel might be there," Tim conceded. "I need to follow up with tech to see if they have her bank account records yet," he said as he pulled out his phone and made a quick call. "They're sending info through to my email. I won't open that now because I'm enjoying this steak far too much to want to pull my laptop out, and I hate checking documents on my phone."

"Hmm," Ashley voiced, her mind active.

"Hmm? That tells me that analysis is going on inside the mind of the fair Ashley," Tim said. "What are you thinking?"

"I keep feeling like we're missing something," she replied. "This young woman doesn't seem like the type of person who just ups and leaves her husband, no matter how jealous he might get." She paused for a while. "We don't yet know what her husband's movements were on that day - Friday. We took his word that he saw her leave that morning and then didn't see her again. How can we confirm that?"

Tim stopped chewing long enough to look at Ashley. He always thought she was sexy, but when she transformed into a full-on analyst, her face took on a different kind of beauty. He never tired of looking at her.

"How can we prove if he did or didn't see her again, do you mean? We'd have to trace where she went, and compare it to a trace of where *he* went," Tim said at last. "Among the documents that have been emailed to me are Flo's phone records. We have seen instances where those kinds of reports include not only details of phone calls and text messages that passed through the phone, but also the GPS location if it was turned on. Hey, we might get lucky there yet. We'll know in twenty minutes when I've finished this."

"Or fifteen, if you eat faster," Ashley said, teasing him again. The only response she got was another Tim smile.

CHAPTER 34

"Alright, let's see what all of this reveals," Tim said as he opened up his laptop. He and Ashley were sitting in her car. Tim smiled at the fact that he could sense her anticipation.

"What are you grinning about?" Ashley asked him.

"You!" Tim replied. "You're chomping at the bit!"

"Are you calling me a horse, Special Agent Tim Moore?" Ashley teased him.

"I wouldn't dare!" Tim said as he burst out laughing.

After a few more minutes, he looked up at Ashley before settling his eyes back onto the laptop screen.

"The phone records only show incoming calls from the same few numbers, mostly on Sunday and mostly from Flo's sister, Kim. There are a few from Daniel, a few from Christine and Stacey, and a couple from her friend Toby."

"Nothing outgoing at all?" Ashley asked.

"No, there's no sign of any outgoing calls," Tim replied. "The report also isn't showing any GPS coordinates for the past week, so she must have had that turned off."

"Hmm, but they can triangulate where the phone has been, can't they?"

"I'll email the tech guys back and see if they can," Tim replied. "In the meantime, we also have her bank account records for the two months up till today. It all looks pretty standard up until Friday morning."

"And what exactly did she do on Friday morning?" Ashley asked.

"Nothing spectacular. Looks like she used her card to buy something at a local café first thing - on her way to work, maybe?" said Tim. "Then it looks like she did some grocery shopping at the local supermarket. That was her last transaction."

"How much?" Ashley asked, resulting in Tim raising his head again, confusion written all over his face. "How much did she spend at the supermarket? Does it look like it was a substantial shopping trip, given the amount, or just picking something up, like milk ... or a toothbrush?"

"One hundred and sixty. I'd say that was a fairly substantial grocery top-up," Tim said as he studied the details in front of him. "What are you thinking?"

"Well, either she bought food that was for their apartment..." Ashley started to say.

"Or she bought enough food to be able to drive away and survive on without having to visit another store again for quite a while," said Tim, finishing the sentence.

"Exactly," said Ashley. "The question is, how do we determine which is right?"

"We go to their apartment and see if there might be a hundred and sixty dollars worth of food in their refrigerator," Tim said.

CHAPTER 35

"Oh," Daniel said, obviously surprised when he opened his apartment door later that afternoon. It wasn't missed on Ashley or Tim that once again, Daniel's eyes revealed evidence of him having been crying for quite some time. "Please come in." He led the agents to his living room and sat down. "Do you have news for me? Have you found her?" he asked, his voice cracking in emotion.

Tim watched Daniel's face. As with their previous visit, it was difficult to truly assess what was real emotion in Daniel, and what might be a well-acted scene. It presented more of a challenge to Tim, and one thing he did absolutely love was a challenge.

"We have nothing to report as yet, Mr. Sloan," Tim said. "We do need to ask you some more questions, however."

Daniel nodded. "Yes, of course."

"When Flo left to go to work on Friday, did she take her car?" Tim asked.

"Yes. Well, I assume so," Daniel replied vaguely. "She always did … *does*."

"You assume so?" Ashley asked him. "You don't know?"

"No," Daniel replied, shaking his head. "She did always take her car to work, so I am confident in assuming she did that day, but I wasn't looking out the window when she left. I didn't actually see her drive away."

"But her car isn't here, I take it," Tim said.

The look on Daniel's face demonstrated that he hadn't

given it any thought. He watched as Daniel jumped up from his seat and walked out into the hallway. When he came back, he spoke.

"Her car keys aren't here," he said.

Tim and Ashley looked at one another.

"And her car isn't either?" Tim dared to ask.

"I haven't been down to the basement, but if her keys aren't here, I'm assuming the car isn't either. It definitely wasn't there when I came home after work on Friday, and I haven't left the apartment since then. She must have left in it. Why are you asking about her car?"

"If we know for certain that she was in her car when she went missing, we can put out a BOLO on it," Ashley said quietly.

"Yes, of course," Daniel replied. "Do you need her registration details?"

"That would be useful, yes," Ashley replied. "Can you take us down to the basement, Mr. Sloan? It would be good if we can be certain that her car isn't here."

Daniel looked at her as if she was crazy, but nodded and grabbed his keys from the hallway on their way out.

"Out of interest, Mr. Sloan, what did your day entail on Friday?" Tim asked as the three of them rode the small elevator downwards.

"I was here at home until eleven-thirty. Then I went and met a friend for lunch," Daniel replied. "After that, I went to my office in town, where I stayed till about five."

Once the elevator doors opened, Daniel led the agents a short distance.

"This is her carpark," he said, pointing at an empty spot.

"She wouldn't park anywhere else in here?" Ashley asked.

"No," Daniel replied. "We pay for two allocated spots that are only for us, like all the tenants in the building do."

"And where is your spot?" Tim asked. When Daniel pointed to the parking space next to what he'd shown as Flo's, Tim moved forward to look around the car parked there. "Yours?"

"Yes, that is my car," Daniel replied.

Although not a crime scene investigator himself, Tim took his time to walk around, looking at the car's surface and underneath at the ground itself.

"What are you looking for?" Daniel asked, slowly growing aware that he might be a suspect himself.

"We are trying to find your wife, Mr. Sloan. Anywhere could be the point that she disappeared from," Ashley said.

"You think ... you think something serious has happened to her? Someone has done something to her, against her will? *Taken* her?" Daniel asked, his facial expression changing up to a look of horror. "But ... she said she wanted time away from me. She's just taking time out ... isn't she?"

Ashley watched as Daniel broke down into tears before her. She knew that weeping wasn't an indication of someone's innocence. Some of the most vicious people she'd put away had put on a pretty good show before they were finally convicted.

"We don't yet know, Mr. Sloan, but we are doing everything we can to find out what has happened to Flo and where she is," Ashley finally said.

The three of them walked back to the elevator and silently went back to the apartment.

"May we look around, Mr. Sloan?" Tim asked.

Daniel looked surprised but eventually nodded.

"Yes, if you think there's anything here that will help you find my wife, please take as long as you need to," he said easily.

It wasn't a usual response, but Tim was glad to not have to go through the process of getting a warrant. As Ashley looked in the bathroom and bedroom, Tim looked through the cupboards and refrigerator in the kitchen.

"You don't have much food, Mr. Sloan," Tim said upon seeing the refrigerator almost empty.

"No, I've tried to get food into me, but I really can't even think about eating right now," Daniel replied. "All I can think about is Flo."

Tim nodded but said nothing more until he and Ashley met up in the living room again.

"Thank you, Mr. Sloan," Ashley said. "Just to double-check, you haven't heard from anyone regarding a ransom demand?" she asked, watching his face as she did so.

"No, I haven't heard from anyone," Daniel said with almost a tone of disgust in his voice.

Tim quickly remembered a question that had burned in his mind when they'd first asked Daniel about his movements on Friday.

"Who was the friend you had lunch with on Friday, Mr. Sloan?" he asked.

Daniel gave him a look of surprise. "Pardon me?"

"Who did you meet for lunch on Friday?" Tim asked again.

"I don't think that is relevant to finding my wife!" Daniel exclaimed, looking either truthfully offended or pretending to do so.

"Please answer the question, Mr. Sloan," Ashley said quietly. "If we are to find your wife, we need to explore all avenues."

"I met my lifetime friend, Tracey."

"Is there any chance she's more than a friend?" Tim asked.

"No!" Daniel replied as he rubbed his eyes with his right thumb and forefinger. "Tracey and I grew up together. There's never been anything romantic if that's what you're implying."

Ashley watched his face. He certainly was an

interesting person to watch the facial expressions of.

"Was Tracey jealous when you married Flo?" she asked.

"No, I don't think so. My marriage hasn't in any way affected my friendship with Tracey. She and Flo get on well," Daniel said before pausing. "Why are you asking about Tracey anyway?"

"As I said, Mr. Sloan, we want to find your wife, and as quickly as possible. If there is any chance that a woman friend of yours was jealous of you having married Flo, we might need to talk to that friend."

"Well, you don't. There's nothing to dig up there, I assure you," Daniel said, sounding incredibly tired.

"Very well. We can show ourselves out," Ashley said as she and Tim moved toward the door.

Before they reached it, Daniel moved toward them and called out.

"Please find her! I can't bear..." he began to say before he broke down once again, weeping loudly.

Tim and Ashley walked out quietly.

Once out of earshot, Ashley turned to Tim.

"He's rather interesting, isn't he. How do you read him and the distress he presents?" she asked as they approached where her car was parked.

"It is difficult reading him," Tim said. "Regardless of that, though, if we want to pursue him as a suspect, we're going to need to find some evidence of something."

"What about the friend?" Ashley asked him.

"I don't know," Tim said, shrugging his shoulders. "Should I get the team back at the office to look into the friend's background?"

Climbing into her car, Ashley was thoughtful.

"No, leave it for now. I think what's more important is finding out more about Flo's movements on that Friday," she said, looking up and down the street.

"Well, we know she went to work and then left again," Tim said. "We know she purchased a fair amount of groceries, and from what I saw of the apartment's kitchen, I don't think she took them home after she purchased them."

"Unless she didn't buy food," Ashley said, prompting Tim to look at her. "I mean, things like toiletries or cleaning products can be pricey, and they wouldn't have been visible in the kitchen necessarily."

"True, but there was almost *no* food in the kitchen," said Tim. "Who would go to a supermarket and not pick at least *some* food up?"

"Hmm, maybe," Ashley replied. "I think it might be worth visiting the supermarket. If we can see their security footage, we might be able to see if Flo went in there alone."

"Yes, that would tell us if she is with someone or not," Tim said in agreement. "They might also be able to tell us what she bought."

"Right!" Ashley said as she started the car engine. "Let's do that then. We're going to work this one out, Timmy Boy. I know it!"

Tim grinned at her. Whenever she addressed him with some form of affection or playfulness, smiling was extremely easy to do.

As they began to move, something caught Tim's eye.

"What about that traffic camera up there? I'm going to call the tech guys and see if they can get footage from that for Friday. I do think we need to know for sure if Flo came home or not," he said before making the call.

Ashley drove onwards, her mind active.

"Okay, that is underway," Tim said after he hung up the call. "That should help us to piece together the movements of Flo on Friday."

"I think it could be interesting to see the movements of Daniel on that day too," Ashley added. "Something is off somewhere. We just need to find out where."

CHAPTER 36

Flo woke up again. Every time she did, she further wished she hadn't. If she was going to die, couldn't it just happen already and be done with? With each waking, she felt giddier than the last time. She put that down to the lack of oxygen.

As she woke further, she considered that the oxygen in the box seemed to be lasting much longer than she would have expected. Not that she knew how long she'd been in there, of course. For all she knew, she might have only been in her current predicament for a few hours. It certainly seemed longer, but with nothing in her pockets that could help her identify time, guessing was all that she could do.

The other aspect that was surprising to her was that despite how long she must have been there, she didn't feel hungry or thirsty. She guessed that meant she hadn't been there very long at all.

She knocked on the wood again. All she heard was the same deep thud as previous times. Part of her wanted to keep hammering her fist against the sides of the box. Part of her wanted to keep screaming as loudly as she could in an effort to get someone's attention. She did neither this time around. What was the point? She wanted to go to sleep again. Hopefully, next time she wouldn't wake up and have to deal with the entire scenario anymore.

Before falling back asleep, she took some time to reflect on her life so far. She was only twenty-five, but she felt like she had grown up since leaving high school.

It was during her later school years that she'd learned just how much she loved writing. Every class she had taken that presented some kind of essay, report, or story to write, Flo had loved and thrived in. She had read fairly constantly since her early childhood years and still loved that. In every book that she picked up, she gained new knowledge as far as word, sentence, and paragraph formations went. It was a skill that she'd never tired of enhancing.

She thought back to some of her best-acknowledged pieces of work. The previous year, she'd won a newspaper reporting award. A few years before that, she'd won an award for a short story she wrote to win some cash. That $1,000 had certainly come in handy right when she'd needed it as a struggling student. In high school, she'd gotten A+ marks fairly often.

Thinking back to her high school years, she laughed out loud. That was right. She'd done an assignment centered around the precise predicament she was now in. Yes! The class had been required to write an essay on how they would feel if they woke up in a coffin. The subject had come up after they'd been required to read some classics, one being Dracula by Bram Stoker.

Flo thought about that time. That year, she'd felt unhappy. Some boy or other had pretended to like her and then publicly humiliated her. At the time, it had felt devastating. It had left Flo wanting to end her life at one point. She was glad she had worked through that with the help of her two older sisters. They were her rock. There had been little she hadn't been able to talk to them about. Even kissing and then sex had been subjects they had talked about together. She had always been aware that what the three of them had as siblings was far more than many other families had.

Into her head popped an image of the classroom that she'd worked on that particular essay in. One thing she'd always found eerie but interesting was her ability to remember events through visualizing the surroundings of them. When she'd written her report on Dracula, and then the essay on how it would feel to wake up in a coffin, she'd been in a class of thirty or so students. She'd sat in the fourth row from the front, two seats along from the wall. In front of her had sat her then best friend, Tammie. That was before Tammie had left town, and left Flo feeling a little lonely. It had all worked out fine, though. Flo also had good friendships established even then with Grant, Toby, Christine, and Stacey.

Tammie. Yes, somewhere along the way, they had lost contact. Flo considered that she really should try and find out how Tammie was doing now. That thought was discarded. In her present predicament, it didn't seem likely that a to-do list was going to be needed.

Flo continued to visualize the entire classroom in her head. She could see the desks as they were set out, and the students that had sat at each one. The only person she still knew who had been in that class with her was Grant. She grinned at the thought of him. When they'd been in high school together, sharing some of the same classes, she had thought he'd had some kind of crush on her. The idea was now ludicrous. He was far too good a friend, and Flo would never have traded that for some kind of romance that probably wouldn't have lasted.

Grant had been in her class when they'd needed to submit an essay on that topic too. She remembered the two of them exchanging their papers so they could each read the other's. Both had laughed at the ridiculous things they'd written. Neither had any idea about life at all at that stage. What they'd written had been just pure imagination.

Given where she was right in the current moment, she thought that funny. She imagined calling Grant to tell him where she was presently lying. That thought made her laugh out loud - until she finally fell asleep once more.

CHAPTER 37

Special Agents Ashley Power and Tim Moore watched over the supermarket's security guard's shoulder as he played back footage from the previous Friday.

"There!" Tim said, pointing as he spotted Flo walking into the supermarket building. "That's her arriving, with a timestamp of … 10:26am."

"Alright," the security guard said as he slowed the footage playback to normal speed. "Let's see what she did."

As they watched, they took note that Flo didn't appear to enter the supermarket with anyone. She also didn't leave with anyone. Of more interest was that in the trolley she pushed around from aisle to aisle, was a growing amount of food products. She grabbed nothing from any non-food aisles at all.

"There's her walking out again at … 11:05am," Ashley said, noting Flo's departure time. "Is there any footage of the carpark?" she asked.

The security guard nodded and changed camera views.

"This is another view of the exit," he said, pointing to the screen.

Ashley and Tim both saw Ashley stop and load up her car before walking the trolley back to the trolley bay, entering her car, and driving off.

Tim didn't say anything out loud, but upon glancing at Ashley, he knew she had also concluded that whatever Flo had purchased, had left the supermarket grounds but hadn't gone back to the apartment.

"Thank you," Ashley said to the security guard when the footage playback was complete. "This has been very helpful."

She and Tim walked out. They now knew when Flo had arrived, when she had left, and what she'd purchased while there. The unknown was where she was, where her car was, or even where the groceries were.

"This is looking more and more like she might have just left her husband, maybe just to make a clean break?" Ashley said to Tim.

Tim shook his head.

"I don't know, Ash. Yes, I can see her wanting to walk away from her husband. The thought of her not responding to calls of her sisters still makes me hesitant about that theory, though. From what everyone has said about her, she just doesn't seem the type to do that."

"We've seen the lengths that women go to in order to escape an abusive husband," Ashley said.

"We have, but even in that, Daniel seems possessive and jealous, but did he physically or verbally abuse her? Nobody we've spoken to has given any indication that he was like that," Tim responded.

"Domestic abuse hardly ever *is* seen by anyone else," Ashley retorted.

Before either could further consider the nature of the missing woman's husband, Tim's phone rang. He promptly answered it. Ashley watched as she saw him respond now and then, and then hung up.

"Tech has managed to get footage from that camera across the street from Sloan's apartment," he said. "It's ready for us to view."

Ashley nodded as she felt her heartbeat increase in anticipation.

"Let's check that out then."

CHAPTER 38

As they sat in Ashley's motel room, she and Tim both felt positive from watching the footage they had been sent. It was only from a street camera, so not exactly exciting, except that it would answer so many questions for them.

On the screen before them, they could see Flo pull out and leave early in the morning. After that, they saw Daniel leave around the time that he'd said he did.

"He did leave close to eleven-thirty then," Tim said as he looked at the time stamp on the footage.

They continued to watch, seeing two other tenants come or go in their vehicles but nothing more. Then they did see two things that were unexpected and captured their attention.

"That's Flo coming home at 12:05pm," Ashley said as they watched Flo's car drive into the apartment basement. A few minutes later, they saw her car leave again. "She's leav..." Ashley started to say before Tim broke off her sentence.

"No, I don't think she is, Ash. Look closer. That's not Flo driving," Tim said.

Both agents leaned in to look closer at the screen.

"Can you stop and enlarge that?" Ashley asked.

Tim obliged, but the image only became grainy.

"Who is that?" asked Ashley.

Tim focused on the male face that sat in the driver's seat.

"Whoever he is, I don't think I've seen him before."

"No, it's not Daniel or any of her friends, is it,"

Ashley said.

"A lover perhaps?" Tim suggested. "This might just be a case of her running away with another man."

Ashley shook her head.

"I don't think so. Look," she said, pointing at the screen. "Flo isn't in the passenger seat. I can't actually see her in the car at all. If they were running away together, surely she would have been sitting with him."

"What if she didn't want people to see them together?" Tim asked.

"I doubt very much she would have suggested they take her car if that were the case," Ashley replied.

Tim agreed, nodding.

"We need to find that car."

"Yes, we do," Ashley said. "Has there been any news since we put that BOLO out?"

Tim shook his head. "Nothing yet."

CHAPTER 39

Three hours later, Ashley and Tim received news they had been waiting for. Flo's car had been found burned out in the carpark of a beach near the neighboring town. On hearing the news, they immediately drove to the location, having been told that crime scene investigators were also on their way there.

As they approached the scene, a member of the crime scene unit approached them.

"Hi, I'm Becca," she said, holding out her hand to both Tim and Ashley.

After both shook it and introduced themselves, Ashley boldly asked the question that was at the very forefront of her mind.

"Is she in it?" she asked.

Becca shook her head.

"No," she said. "We need to do a full examination of the car, but I can already tell you that there's no body in it. At this stage, it looks like it was just dumped and torched."

Tim's mind worked quickly.

"Is there any chance you can tell if there was any food in it?" he asked.

Becca gave a look of curiosity. "Food?"

"Yes," Ashley said. "Our missing woman was seen on camera footage buying a large amount of food from the supermarket. We're not sure how, but finding out where she took that might be of importance. We don't yet know if she dropped the groceries home or if they were still in the car."

"Oh, I see," Becca said, nodding. "Well, that is something I should be able to tell you once we get some investigation results back, but right now, pretty much everything is just one big black mess."

Ashley handed her a card.

"Can you please call us as soon as you find out if the groceries were in it at the time of torching or not? It looked like a substantial grocery shop so…"

Becca nodded again and smiled sadly.

"I can do that for you," she said.

"With urgency?" Tim asked, giving his best grin.

"Of course," Becca replied before moving away to return to the remnants of the car.

Tim and Ashley looked on, watching pieces here and there be gathered up and bagged for testing. After a few minutes, they moved away.

"There's a bench seat down there," Tim said, pointing toward the beach. "Let's go sit down and think about all of this for a bit."

Ashley nodded but said nothing. Her mind was busy.

Once they sat, Tim began recapping what they'd learned so far.

"Okay, we know that Flo went to work. We know she went and bought groceries. We know she went home," he started. "We also know that a man drove her car out of her apartment complex, and somehow it ended up here and was set on fire."

"Right," Ashley said, nodding. "We also know that Daniel had left the apartment building by the time Flo returned."

"Unless he was aware of that camera and somehow doubled back, entering a back door or something," Tim suggested.

"True, but I don't think that guy in Flo's car looked anything like Daniel Sloan. Do you think it could be him?"

"It didn't look like him to me," Tim replied. "That

isn't to say that he didn't have anything to *do* with that guy taking the car."

"And we still don't know if Flo was in the car when it was taken," said Ashley. "Was she in it, or was she already back in the apartment?"

"We need more information about where the car went between that apartment and here," Tim said.

"Or information about who was in that car," Ashley added. She was silent for a long moment before she spoke again.

CHAPTER 40

"That's our confirmation that the groceries most likely weren't in the car when it was set alight," Tim said as he hung up his phone and looked at Ashley. "We do now have the name of another person who was in that car, but there's no way to know *when* he was in the car, so it might not mean anything."

"Okay," Ashley said as she nodded. "Who was it?"

Tim read details off his laptop screen.

"It's a guy with a record the length of your arm, but only theft charges. His name is Noah Cameron."

"Do we have contact details for him?" Ashley asked.

"Yeah, he lives not far from here," Tim replied.

Without hesitation, Ashley began moving towards the carpark again. Ten minutes later, they pulled up to a run-down house with a large yard full of old car bodies. As they climbed out of the car, Tim and Ashley both felt wary. Regardless, they moved up to the front door and knocked. When the door opened, they were greeted by the man they recognized from the mug shot they'd been provided with.

"Mr. Cameron, I am Special Agent Ashley Power…" she began. That was as far as she got before Noah bolted out the door and began to run toward the street.

"Stop!" Tim said as he began pursuit. It was only seconds before he leaped forward, pulling Noah down to the ground and securing handcuffs on his wrists.

"I ain't done nothing wrong!" Noah yelled, over and over.

"Good, then there's no harm in us having a chat, is

there," Tim said as he pulled Noah to his feet.

Ashley walked up to them and looked Noah in the eyes.

"Where were you on Friday morning, Mr. Cameron?" she asked.

"Nowhere," came the reply, a menacing tone in it.

"Really? Are you sure? Because a woman is missing. She might be dead. That would mean a murder charge, and it looks like you were in her car," Tim said.

"I ain't committed no murder!" the man insisted. "Are you crazy? I never hurt anyone."

"Well, then, how about you tell us what we want to know," Ashley prompted him.

After some time holding his tough stance, Noah folded a little.

"Okay!" he said. "I was in the next town over and had to get home to my girl, so I took a car. It was there, running with the keys in the ignition and the door wide open, so I took it."

"And?" Tim pushed.

"And … look, I saw a running car in this basement area, so I jumped into it and took it. When I got up the road, I noticed groceries in the back seat. My first thought was to give them to my Ma, so I drove back here and unloaded it all for her. Then I took the car to the beach and set it alight."

"Why?" Ashley asked. "Why did you set it alight?"

"Because it was fun!" came the snide reply.

"Okay," Ashley said, nodding. "Now, what about the woman?"

"What woman?" Noah asked.

"The woman whose car you stole."

"I never seen no woman," the young man replied. "I walked in there, and the car was there, engine running and the driver door wide open. I jumped in it and got the hell out of there. If there was any woman around, I didn't see her. I swear!"

"Nobody yelled out at you when you drove it out of the basement area?" Ashley asked.

"No," Noah said, shaking his head again. "Look, I steal things. Ain't no point in me denying that, but I don't hurt people," he continued.

"Is your mother home now?" Ashley asked.

"Yeah, she's inside," Noah replied, nodding towards the house.

"You go in. I'll stay with this one out here so he can't taint what she says," Tim said.

Ashley nodded and turned to go toward the house. Upon knocking on the open door, she heard a woman's voice call out to come in.

"Mrs. Cameron?" Ashley asked when an older woman came into view.

"Yes. Who are you?"

"I am Special Agent Ashley Power."

"No!" the woman said, looking like she would collapse. "Please don't take him away again. He takes things, but he's not a bad boy."

"It's alright, Mrs. Cameron," said Ashley. "We aren't here about any theft. We're trying to locate a woman who's been missing for almost a week."

The woman looked hard and closed off all of a sudden.

"What's that got to do with us?"

"We think your son may have been driving her car last Friday," Ashley replied. "Do you remember that day?"

"I do," the woman said. "My boy drove a car into the driveway, and it was loaded with food. He told me he'd taken the car to get home from the next town. I asked him if he'd stolen the food. He said he hadn't. Reckoned it was just in the car," she said, a look of sadness coming over her face. "Did he do it? Did he steal all that food from a supermarket?"

Ashley shook her head, feeling sorry for the woman.

"No, we believe that he stole the car with the food already inside it."

The woman hung her head.

"And now he'll go away again for stealing the car," she said.

"About that, I cannot say, Mrs. Cameron. Right now, we are only concerned with finding this missing woman. Is there anything you can tell me that your son might have mentioned to you about the woman who owned the car he stole on Friday?"

"No, he never mentioned any woman," the woman replied. "Said he'd found it open and with the engine running, like it was ready and waiting for him to steal it. He didn't mention anyone being around or anything. I told him it sounded a little too easy, but he said that maybe it was meant to be. He knew we had no food in the pantry. He saw it as a gift from God to make sure we could eat."

Ashley listened and only nodded. While she didn't doubt that there were grounds to take Noah away and charge him with stealing and destroying the car, for the moment, all she wanted to concentrate on was finding Flo, preferably alive.

"Well, thank you, Mrs. Cameron," Ashley said and began to walk out. Once out on the path out front, she called out to Tim. "Uncuff him."

Tim didn't question her instruction. As he undid the cuffs, Ashley walked up to Noah.

"Don't leave town. We might still need to question you more," she said.

Noah held up his hands, knowing he was fortunate that they weren't taking him away then and there.

"Look, I stole that car, I kept the food that was in it, and then I set it on fire," he said. "I didn't see any woman or *anyone* around the car when I took it, I swear."

"I believe you," Ashley said, nodding. "Tell me this, though. Was there a purse, a phone, or anything personal in the car?"

Noah looked down and then back up into Ashley's face.

"Yeah, there was a handbag and it had a wallet and a phone in it."

Ashley dreaded asking the next question but knew she had to.

"Do you have them still?"

"Hang on," Noah said as before he walked toward the house.

Tim and Ashley both suspected Noah might bolt out the back door, but to his credit, he came back with a handbag in his hands.

"I gave this to my ma too," he said, reluctantly handing it over. "The phone is in there too."

"And the wallet?" Tim asked, not expecting any good news to come from that question. "Money?"

"I gave the money to my ma," Noah replied. "It's already gone. The wallet itself is in there, though."

"How much was in it?" Ashley asked. When Noah looked confused, she pushed harder. "Noah, this is important. Was it a small amount or a lot?"

"There was a fifty dollar note and a few smaller notes. It wasn't like thousands or anything," Noah replied. "Probably sixty-five bucks, maybe."

"Okay, Noah," Tim said. "We can't guarantee you aren't going to get into trouble for all of this, but I can tell you that today, we are only interested in finding this woman. We won't be alerting anyone today to the bad decisions you made last Friday."

Noah looked ashamed but said nothing more as Tim and Ashley left.

Partway down the road, Tim turned to Ashley.

"Should we believe what he told us about not having seen anyone when he took the car?"

Ashley shrugged her shoulders.

"As dishonest as he obviously is in stealing what isn't

his, I do think he might have been honest in saying that the car was running when he took it," she said. "He seems more like a guy who makes stupid decisions, but he does seem to care about his mother, and sometimes that says a lot about their natures, doesn't it."

Tim wasn't so sure but said nothing. In truth, his ability to read people's vibes also told him that Noah had just grown up a mixed-up kid with some weird attraction to stealing.

"It's odd though, that the car would have been running," Tim said.

"Yes, and that the groceries were in it," Ashley added. "If I lived in a place with a basement carpark, and I lived upstairs, I most likely wouldn't get out of my car and go and unlock the apartment, then go back and bring the groceries up. And I definitely wouldn't have left the car running."

Tim thought about the way Noah had described finding the car.

"Do you think she could have been grabbed as she got out of the car?"

"Hmm," Ashley pondered. "So Flo drives into her basement carpark, then climbs out of the driver seat, moving toward opening the passenger door to get the groceries out..."

"But why leave the car running?" Tim asked. "Who would do that?"

"Nobody, if they were just going to unload groceries," replied Ashley. "What if someone took Flo and then turned the key again to make sure that someone noticed the car was there, easy to be taken?"

"Okay, someone takes Flo and then, thinking ahead to when it would be brought to the attention of law enforcement, they set up things so that the car will be stolen. That gives them a bit more time to do whatever they plan to do while we're chasing whoever stole the car," Tim said. "The thing I don't like about that is that we still don't know where Flo *is*. She wasn't in the car when Noah took it. If someone took her, they did it in that timeframe between when we saw Flo drive the car into the apartment block and when we saw Noah drive it out. It's not much time."

"Plus, we also don't know if she ever left the apartment block," Ashley said.

Tim looked at her, his mind awash with new possibilities.

"You think she might be still in the building somewhere?" he asked.

"Maybe," Ashley said, nodding. "We need to look at that street camera footage again."

CHAPTER 41

Tim and Ashley watched the footage from the street camera over and over. They watched from the Thursday night, right through to the time when Daniel Sloan returned home just after 5pm on the Friday.

"What aren't we seeing? We've seen Flo go home on the evening after seeing her friends. We've seen her then leave for work the following morning, and return home after work," Ashley said. As she worded the summary in such a way, Tim's mind took a different route of thinking.

"*Did* we see her return home after work?" he asked.

Ashley looked at him, not sure where he was going in his line of thought.

"We saw on the street camera…"

"Her *car* return home after work," Tim finished. "Look at the footage. The camera faces on an angle that enabled us to see into the car as it *exited* the building. It also enabled us to see the car enter the building, but when we see it go in, it's not possible to see who was *driving* the car."

After a long while, Ashley spoke.

"We know that she was in the supermarket, and she bought all that food," she said.

"We also know that, assuming Noah was telling the truth, when he stole the car, the food was in it," said Tim.

"Right," Ashley said. "We know, then, that Flo did walk out of the supermarket and successfully load her groceries into her car."

"What if somewhere between her loading her car and getting home, she met someone, and *they* drove her car back to the apartment. Once there, they left the car running and then exited the building, looping back around somehow to go back to wherever they'd left her," Tim offered.

"But who, and why?" Ashley asked, studying his face. "If that is what's happened, is Flo a part of it?"

"Hmm, but then why would she buy the food if she was only going to walk away from it? Wouldn't she have taken it with her in the other person's car if she was running away?" Tim asked.

"Maybe, unless she wanted to get away and make it *look* like she'd been abducted," Ashley said.

"Back to the Flo running away theory, huh?" Tim asked. "I don't like it. Something about that option just doesn't work for me, I have to say. How can we prove or disprove it?"

"Media," Ashley said. "We haven't yet let the TV channels run with this missing person story. Let's get that set up and run it. If she's out there in hiding somewhere, seeing the distress she's causing her sisters, at least, might force her to come out and face what she's done."

"And if she was taken against her will?"

"Then her abductor will know we are closing in on them," Ashley said.

CHAPTER 42

Both agents sat in Ashley's motel room the next day as the first news report was aired.

'Police are calling for any sightings of a local woman, Fiona Sloan,' the reporter said as a photo of Flo appeared on the screen. 'Also known as Flo, the young woman was last seen on the morning of last Friday, in the Lo-Cost Supermarket.'

"Well, at least her photo is out there now," Tim said as the reporter delivered essential details about Flo's appearance and background. "Someone will have seen or heard something, no doubt."

"Here's hoping, because I feel lost in this case, Tim," Ashley revealed.

"Every case has that moment when we question if we'll ever solve it, Ash. So far, there hasn't been one that we haven't," Tim said with his usual cocky confidence.

"That doesn't mean one won't come along that we can't solve. It doesn't mean that *this* one might not be solvable!" Ashley exclaimed.

Tim reached out and placed his arms around her, providing support to her while remaining careful in how close he got. He'd already learned Ashley had a line that she was comfortable for him to be on one side of, but not wanting him to cross. It had taken a while for him to figure out where exactly that line lay, but the odd comforting hug seemed to be on her acceptable behavior list.

Ashley accepted the unspoken offer of a hug. Most of the time, she felt confident in the cases she was assigned.

At other times, when she began to experience the frustration of not feeling she was achieving as much as she should on a case, her confidence took a dive. In those times, she was particularly glad to have Tim as a partner. After having worked a fair few cases together, not only had they grown comfortable with each other, but he also seemed to have developed insight into her comfort levels, and her emotions. It made working with a member of the opposite sex much easier when they didn't assume she was available to them romantically or sexually just because she was a single woman.

When she pulled away, a new consideration came to mind.

"What if the sisters are covering for her, helping her to get away?" she asked out loud.

"You think they've been lying to Daniel and to us?" Tim asked, surprised by the possibility. "You think this might all be some kind of cover-up to help Flo get away from Daniel?" he asked. Both remained quiet as they considered the idea. "There's nothing on Flo's phone records to say she's been in contact with them. Oh, but wait," he said upon contemplation. "We already know that she doesn't have her phone on her. If she was going to talk to them, she'd have to have purchased another phone. Did she buy one at the supermarket?"

"No, the receipt copy we obtained didn't show a phone on it. She could have bought one anytime, though, either before that supermarket visit, or after," Ashley replied.

Tim pulled out his phone and made a call directly.

"The tech guys are looking at calls in and out of both sisters' phones since Friday morning," he said after he hung up. "Even if Flo has a burner phone, there'll be records of her calls to them."

"Unless they also have burner phones," Ashley said.

"Okay, wait, Ash. We are getting further and further away from the assumption that Flo was taken against her will. Even if this new scenario is real - or any alternate scenario along those lines - we need to focus primarily on finding her," he said, his voice serious. "There could be a young woman out there, in trouble but still alive."

"Yes, let's go through this timeline again," Ashley said, standing and beginning to pace.

After going through their notes of Flo's movements according to the different snippets of security footage they'd looked at, Ashley and Tim took some time to think about what they might have missed.

"There's quite a gap, isn't there?" Ashley asked. "I mean, she left the supermarket carpark at 11:10am. We know her car pulled into the apartment building basement at 12:05pm. Where did she go between those times? I can't imagine it takes an hour to get from the grocery store to her home."

"Good question. That's assuming that it *was* Flo driving her car, of course," Tim said. "I mean, if you went to a supermarket and bought food, including frozen foods, which we know she did, wouldn't you want to go straight home and at least get the frozen stuff into the freezer?" he asked.

Ashley nodded.

"I would," she said, thoughtful. "That opens up the question of whether something happened to her between leaving the supermarket and arriving home. That's the issue, isn't it. We don't know if she *did* arrive home or if someone else drove her car there."

"Let's go and look at that carpark basement again," Tim said suddenly, standing up. "No matter who drove Flo's car into that building, they had to get out again if they didn't drive her car."

"Which we know they didn't because Noah did that," said Ashley. "Okay," she agreed as she quickly grabbed and put on her coat.

With the anticipation of finding a clue, the two of them made their way quickly to the apartment block and entered the basement carpark.

"It's weird that there's no security on a building that caters to such high profile and wealthy tenants, isn't it," Tim said quietly. "I think I'd prefer to live somewhere that at least has some kind of card swipe access."

"Me too, but you're right. It is odd that Daniel Sloan would live somewhere not so secure. He must be able to afford to live in the highest security penthouse in the city," Ashley replied. "Then again, what is normal about Mr. Sloan?"

"He hasn't won you over yet, huh?" Tim asked, smiling while knowing full well he was cheekily teasing his partner. The look Ashley gave him in response made him laugh out loud. "Noted!"

Once inside, they parked in Flo's carpark.

"I guess Daniel finally left the apartment then," Ashley said, noting the absence of Daniel's car in his park.

"Looks like it," Tim responded as he looked around. "Right. Let's go for a wander around this place. I want to see how many exits there are."

They walked around the inside areas of the outer walls of the carpark. They were just about to arrive back at the entrance when Tim spoke up.

"Look," he said, walking directly towards what looked like a security officer's office.

"There's nobody here," Ashley said. "I don't think there was the last time we came here either."

"No," Tim said, trying the door and finding it open. Walking in, he walked briskly to the far wall. "Look," he said. Reaching down to press on the large bar, he easily opened what looked like a fire door. "Here's our exit point," Tim continued as he and Ashley walked out into the sunshine on the other side of the building.

Ashley stopped where she was and looked all around. Her hope that there would be a security camera on the side of the building was lost. There was no building security in sight. As she turned and faced the street and the buildings on the other side of it, however, she realized hope was not all lost. Across the street was a service station. With the fuel tanks outside, it looked like just the kind of place that would appreciate security cameras.

Tim watched her face and let his eyes follow where hers remained. He grinned at her.

"Shall we?" he asked, already feeling like they must be getting closer. He hoped so anyway. As every hour passed, he continued to think about Flo more and more. There were always reasons why a case should be solved, but when it was a case about a missing person, he truly felt the urgency in finding them before it was too late.

Entering the service station, Ashley and Tim were forced to wait several minutes while the attendant behind the counter served the few customers that were in line. Ashley didn't mind at all. The busier the station was, the more likely it was that their security was good. She hoped so anyway.

"Hello," Tim said to the attendant when they were finally the only people in the small store area. "I'm Special Agent Moore, and this is Special Agent Power. We noticed you have a security camera out front," he continued, resulting in the attendant nodding. "Is there any chance we can see your footage from last Friday morning?"

The attendant looked worried but replied.

"I'll need to talk to my boss," she said. "Sorry, he deals with all that stuff. I just serve here."

"Yes, of course," Tim replied, delivering a smile. "Could you call him for us, please?"

As the attendant made the phone call, Ashley and Tim looked out from the service station and toward the large apartment building. Now that they knew where the discreet fire door was, it was easy to see. It hadn't caught their eye on their previous visit, it was so well hidden from the street.

"He's on his way. He'll be here in a few minutes," the attendant called out to Ashley and Tim.

A short time later, they stood with the service station owner.

"Hi, you want to see security footage? Is there some kind of problem?" the owner asked, somewhat nervously.

"No, not with your service station, Mr....?" Ashley asked, smiling at him.

The owner held out his hand to her. "Anderson. Bob Anderson."

"Mr. Anderson," Ashley said as she shook his hand and nodded. "What we are hoping to see is the view from here to over there," she said, turning and pointing at the apartment block across the road.

The owner looked surprised. Even though he still had a nervous stance about him, he nodded.

"Yep, I should be able to provide that. Come this way to my office and let's take a look," he said, leading Tim and Ashley through the shop area and out the back. After they all entered a small office, the owner sat at a desk, switched on the computer monitor, and began using his mouse to click on folders. "Do you know what date you are wanting to look at?" he asked finally.

Tim gave the date and time details. The owner clicked on various files according to date and time stamp, while Ashley and Tim looked over his shoulder.

Both agents were relieved to see that the door was in perfect view of the service station camera. It made Ashley's heart pound. She was hopeful for the first few minutes of looking. Slowly, her hope began to fade. Her optimism had almost completely disappeared when she heard Tim speak excitedly.

"Look!" he said. When Ashley looked closely at the screen, she saw the door open, and a person walk out of it. "That's at ... 12:06pm," Tim continued, his voice clearly showing his excitement as he grinned at Ashley. He took a moment to write the time down in a notebook he carried with him at all times.

"Is it possible for us to get a copy of that, Mr. Anderson?" Ashley asked.

The owner smiled at her. The smile would have made her feel nervous if she'd been alone, with its creepy vibe.

"Yep, I can just put it onto one of these," the owner replied as he reached into a shelf beside his desk and retrieved a CD. "I hardly even use these things anymore, so I don't know why I keep them, but I guess I was just meant to have some handy today," he said.

Once the copy was complete, the owner placed the CD into a case and handed it to Ashley.

"I hope that helps with whatever you're working on."

"Thank you. This will help us a lot," Ashley said before she and Tim moved to walk out.

"What is it that you're hoping to find out?" the owner called out.

In response, Ashley turned and smiled at him once more.

"Can we contact you again if we have any questions, Mr. Anderson?" she asked, avoiding his question entirely.

"Yeah, of course," the owner responded without getting up from his seat.

"Thanks," Tim said, encouraging Ashley out the door.

Once out on the street, Tim looked at the apartment building.

"There's no way the guy on this footage *entered* through that door," he confirmed after doing a quick assessment to see if it was a possibility.

"No, I'm feeling hopeful that the timeframe that this guy was walking out, makes him the person who was driving Flo's car when it entered the apartment carpark," Ashley replied. "And I think you're right. He brought it back and left it open for someone to steal, purely to send the cops on a wild goose chase while he did whatever he wanted to do to her."

"But why bring it back here? If someone took her, why not just leave the car open and running wherever they did that?" Tim asked as he considered the possibility.

Ashley thought for a moment before replying.

"If he took Flo somewhere out in public, he probably wanted everything to look as normal as possible. Walking away from a car that is wide open and running would catch someone's attention. This way, he's achieved the objective of sending us on a wild goose chase as we look for the car, but it's far more discreet."

Tim nodded and looked sharply at Ashley.

"You don't hold out hope that she's okay, do you," he said.

Ashley smiled at him sadly.

"I'm not ready to give up on Flo yet, but we do have to be ready for anything. That's always the way, unfortunately."

Together they made their way around the side of the building until they could walk into the basement carpark via the main entrance again. Once inside, they sat inside Ashley's car for a few minutes before she started the engine.

"We need to get this footage to tech so they can run it through facial recognition. It's hard to see the person's face with that cap on, but maybe the tech guys can do their magic," Tim said, starting up his laptop. "Hopefully, we'll get lucky, and his face will be in the system."

"Fingers crossed," Ashley said, doubt showing in her voice.

"What are you uncertain about?" Tim asked her.

"Well, the thing is that the footage doesn't show us anything to do with Flo, does it," Ashley replied. "I mean, we can see a guy leave, but he isn't leaving with *her*. Even if we identify him, are we going to be able to place him *with* her somehow?"

Tim watched her face as she spoke.

"You're doubting yourself quite a bit on this case. It's not like you. Are you okay?" he asked sincerely.

"Yeah," Ashley replied as she smiled at him. "This one's getting to me a bit. I think it's mainly because we don't yet know if Flo is alive or not. I just keep thinking that the longer we're taking to solve this and find her, the more likely it is that she won't be alive by the time we get to her."

"Stop thinking like that, Ash," Tim responded. "We're definitely getting closer. I can feel it. Don't forget that Flo's face is out there on the news now too. That's bound to bring in some attention. Sometimes, people's memories are jogged when they see a face on the news. You know that."

"Yeah, I know," Ashley said. "You're right."

"Of course, I am. Now, surely it's time to eat," Tim said to lighten the mood.

The trick worked. Ashley was prompted into letting out a chuckle as she grinned at him.

"Okay. That sounds good. What do you feel like?" she asked.

"I really liked that steakhouse we went to," Tim said as he grinned, making Ashley laugh out loud.

"Really? Was it the steakhouse, or the steakhouse *waitress* that you liked so much?" she teased him.

"Actually, it was the *food* that I liked!" Tim exclaimed as he laughed, relieved to see his partner look happier. "And that's enough of your cheekiness, Special Agent Power!"

Ashley grinned at him. Nothing more was said about the case as they remained silent on their way to the restaurant, both entirely absorbed in their individual thoughts.

CHAPTER 43

Relaxing over a good meal provided a challenge for Ashley. She appreciated the good food in front of her, and was determined to eat it. As she ate bite after bite, however, she hardly tasted the flavors of the food. Her mind was too focused on Flo. She'd worked on abduction cases before. She'd also worked on cases where the missing person had turned out to be on the run from an abusive situation. There was so much open on the current case that she found it difficult to be certain which possible scenario was in play. Had Flo been abducted, taken somewhere against her will, or had she gone away on her own accord, going into hiding to either avoid her husband or be with someone else?

"I can almost see your mind working," Tim said as he watched her. Even he was finding it difficult to switch his mind off from the case. "Is there anything in particular that has you so absorbed?" he asked.

"No, I'm just thinking over everything we know and everything we've guessed," Ashley replied.

Just then, Tim's phone rang. He promptly answered it, talked for a few minutes, and then hung up. There was no happiness or humor in his facial expression, which said a lot.

"Oh, no. Please tell me they haven't found her..." Ashley said, dread filling her heart.

"No!" Tim exclaimed. "No, that was head office. They were able to run that guy through facial recognition, but nothing came up," he said.

"What about social media?" Ashley asked, hopeful.

"No, they searched that too," Tim replied. "This guy isn't on anything, the database reckons."

"He's older then," Ashley said. "Well, *maybe* older. Generally, it's the next generation up that hasn't joined some kind of social media, isn't it."

"Sometimes," Tim agreed. "That isn't a proven or reliable theory, though."

"True," Ashley responded. "Okay, where do we go from here?" she asked, her doubt creeping in once more.

"Well, first we finish these delicious meals," Tim replied, smiling sadly. "Then we hope that someone will see Flo on the TV and call in their sighting."

CHAPTER 44

With each cycle of waking, Flo then wanted to sleep longer than she had been. The problem was that there was no longer any context of time to work from. Certainly, she felt like she was sleeping and then waking remarkably frequently. She knew she was young and healthy, but she was still surprised that her body was doing so well in the situation she was in. For the duration that she'd been in the box, she hadn't been able to move much at all. From her experience in simply trying to lie in bed longer on the weekends, she knew that her body always reached a point where it was restless. The few times she'd persisted in trying to stay in bed on those mornings, her body had then changed from restless to aching, with her muscles telling her clearly that she needed to move. It was odd that she'd moved even less since she'd woken the first time in the box, and yet her body didn't seem to be moaning about it at all.

It was frustrating that she kept waking up. She wished for death to come and just take her. She hadn't yet lived much of a life, but she couldn't see that getting out of the box and having an opportunity to continue with life was likely. So far, she hadn't heard anything or anyone. It seemed like she was in a bubble, away from the general population.

In the realization that she wasn't tired, and therefore unlikely to quickly fall asleep again, Flo let her mind take her back to different moments in her life once more. She thought about her parents, now long gone from her life. Thinking about them was something she could only tolerate in very small portions. It was too painful, that particular subject.

She turned her mind to the men who had passed through her life. The first guy she'd dated, she couldn't even remember the name of now. After he'd humiliated her, she'd made a point to forget him. She smiled at the thought that she must have succeeded in doing that since she sure couldn't remember what he'd been called.

Also at that time had been the growing sense that her good friend, Grant, had developed a crush on her. At that age, it had seemed a romantic notion that he might have done so. She'd never approached him during those years to confront him. Her previous experience with the asshole she'd been humiliated by had left her unable to speak to guys for months out of fear of rejection and further embarrassment.

Now, so many years later, she was glad that nothing had ever happened between her and Grant. He'd turned out to be one of her closest friends. They'd had some amazing conversations over the years. She'd never been sure how he would turn out as a man. Most of the time, he was conventional, following the same trends as everybody else. At other times, he'd been a bit radical, challenging friends, family, and society as a whole. Flo was glad his nature had evened out in recent months. He'd owned his own home for a couple of years and quietened down a lot. He was still one of her closest friends but once upon a time, they'd spent a fair bit of one on one time together. Their ability to talk had always been amazing, leaving them chatting for hours sometimes.

Not that it was like that now, of course. Now, she and each of her four close friends all had such busy lives that they hardly ever spent one on one time together. That was the change in becoming a grown-up, she supposed. The times of hanging out with a good friend for hours and hours on end, day after day, just didn't exist anymore. That kind of time investment was now centered on partners instead.

With a natural progression, her thoughts moved from Grant to her ex-boyfriend, Brent. She'd met him when she'd first left high school. That had been a case of literally running into someone, as they'd collided upon walking around the same corner but in different directions. Throughout her time with Daniel, Flo had purposely not thought about Brent. It had felt like a betrayal to even let him enter her thoughts. Now, she guessed it didn't matter so much.

Brent had been the first guy who'd enabled her to discover what it felt like to be considered attractive. From the very first moment she'd met him, he'd gone out of his way to shower her with attention, working hard to keep her in his life after they'd first met. That he'd also found the need to go and find himself another woman was always a painful thought to Flo. If he'd wanted someone else, why hadn't he just let her go so that she could have found her own happiness elsewhere? No, it wasn't that he'd wanted someone else. It was that he'd wanted several women in his life. He'd never said as much, but that was the conclusion Flo had come to. Sometimes, she felt it was such a pity. The two of them had gotten on so well, in her mind anyway. Perhaps that was the problem. Perhaps he hadn't considered them well-matched at all.

She thought back to just before she met Daniel. Brent had spent six months chasing her up, just as if nothing negative had ever happened between them. She knew as she'd received every text message from him, no matter how small, that she was no longer interested. In being dishonest and deceitful toward her, Brent had completely lost her. That was how the universe wanted it to be, she was sure. Otherwise, she wouldn't have met Daniel.

Ah, Daniel, she thought to herself. He'd pursued her with as much vigor as Brent had. The biggest difference that came to light in those early times was how they connected physically, of course. Sex had been nice enough with Brent. With Daniel, it was on another level. He'd also shown her the charm of a true gentleman, and the independence that could work without either party cheating.

She took a moment to wonder if he *had* cheated on her, either before their wedding or since. Maybe that was what drove him over the edge in doing to her what he'd done. Maybe he'd met someone who he wanted to be with more, and getting rid of Flo was the only way he could be with the other woman.

In the confines of her current situation, it was easy for her writer's mind to take over her internal dialogue. Ever the one for finding a story, she considered Daniel having found someone else. Maybe it wouldn't be Daniel who had disposed of her in that case. Maybe it would be the other woman! Flo let her mind wander. She knew she was running purely fictional scenarios through her mind, but it was refreshing to think about something other than the predicament she was in.

Although she tried to remember how she'd ended up in the box, she couldn't recollect it happening. In all honesty, she couldn't remember much at all. Work was on her mind. There was a certainty that she'd gone into work and delivered a final copy of a report she'd been requested to complete. That was secure in her memory. Anything after that seemed to be missing.

For a moment, she wondered if anyone was looking for her. She had good friends, but she only saw them once a month, and she'd done that recently. She had two sisters, but she saw them only on Sundays. She had no idea if it was Sunday yet. If it was, were they worried about her and wondering where she was? Then there was Daniel, her loving husband. Would he wonder where she was - or did he already know? That was where her focus lay in wondering what had happened to her. Daniel had been so sweet, caring, and loving at the start. He'd worked so hard to win her heart.

Overall, even in considering what he'd done to her to put her in her current situation, she couldn't deny that she'd loved Daniel. He had so many good qualities, and generally, he was always good to her. It was only those few moments that tainted everything - those times when he showed a jealous side that wasn't attractive at all. It hurt Flo considerably, knowing that her husband didn't trust her. Trust was such a big thing. She didn't understand why he'd even bothered to marry her. He knew before proposing that she had men in her life who were friends or colleagues. If that was such a difficult thing for him to accept, why didn't he break off their relationship and go find a woman who didn't have men so close in their life?

Believing there was no resolution to her many questions - nor might there ever be - she sighed. She'd been warned by all those who loved her that things might not end well with Daniel. She had to concede that there was a good chance they'd been right. The little bit of his over the top behavior that she'd seen on those few occasions of jealousy, had grown into something huge. He'd been driven to distraction, doing something drastic to her. That must have been what had happened, and that was what she would accept for as long as she lived.

Flo laughed. As long as she lived. Just how long was that going to be, she wondered.

CHAPTER 45

In a small shed at the back of a property that bordered the nearby forest, a computer monitor was turned on. All day long, the user had been anticipating his daily fix of watching what was happening inside the coffin. Now, he had to wait no more.

He settled into the old chair that he'd taken from the dining room of his home months earlier. It hadn't been so comfortable then. Now it was well worn in. Hours upon hours of sitting in it, planning his move and then watching what was happening on the screen, had helped it finally mellow and yield. For years, that chair had been sitting inside the house, untouched, never sat on. In his opinion, everything that wasn't used wasn't loved. That rule applied to any household item. It also applied to people and the skills that people had.

As he focused on the screen, he felt excited. It had taken more than a year of planning in his head and on paper, putting into place everything he would need for what he wanted to do. So many scenarios had passed through his mind in those beginning stages. The various hypothetical situations had resulted in his plan changing a lot from its inception to actual fruition. That was good. He'd needed to calm his excitement about what he'd needed to do to make his dreams a reality.

The infrared camera had been the best idea of all. Being able to use night vision capability had been vital. After all, what he'd wanted to do wouldn't have been even half as much fun if he couldn't watch it.

It had taken time to get everything working so that

the object of his desire could remain alive while going through the experience. He'd toyed with this idea and that. There had been small alterations made to the coffin and the setup here and there. When he'd worked out a system and set up that suited his plan perfectly, he'd been elated. It was more than a dream come true.

It was destiny.

CHAPTER 46

"Do you think someone might be lying?" Ashley asked Tim as they sat in her car, enjoying a takeaway lunch while overlooking the ocean.

Tim finished chewing his mouthful of fried noodles and looked up at her.

"It's *always* possible that someone's lying, Ash," he said. "Do you have someone in mind?"

"No," Ashley replied. "If any of the people we've interviewed are involved, they've covered their tracks well. Now that we've checked phone records of all her family and friends, we know there's nothing in there anywhere that is out of the ordinary. We also know, from Flo's bank accounts, that she hasn't done anything financial since the morning she disappeared."

"True," Tim said, nodding. "We also know that Daniel did leave the apartment when he said he did, *and* he returned when he said he did. Plus, his alibi checked out. He was at the restaurant with someone over lunchtime that day."

"Yes, it was another woman, though. Do you think we need to talk to her? Maybe there's something more going on there than we've anticipated," Ashley said.

Tim considered what she was saying.

"We know from looking at the restaurant security cameras that they ate lunch together. There was nothing in the footage that suggested they were anything more," he replied. "They didn't touch, except that brief hug before saying goodbye. There was nothing about their body language that suggested there was more between them. Even if there was, the time works well to prove Daniel wasn't at the apartment block when Flo's car returned. We also know that it wasn't him who snuck out that fire door."

"Yeah, but is it a little *too* perfect, do you think?" Ashley asked. "It seems like a relatively brief timeframe that Flo disappeared in…"

"Is it?" Tim questioned. "We know that she walked out of the supermarket and got into her car around 11:10am. That's the last that we've seen of Flo herself. Maybe she was in the car when it returned to the apartment, but maybe she wasn't."

Ashley looked at him, studying his face as her mind worked.

"But where did she go?" she asked. "Where *would* she go, if not home?"

"Possibly, her sisters could answer that. They must know her better than anyone," Tim said. "Well, maybe. I guess any of her close friends could also know if she has a place she likes to go to. Most people have somewhere that they head to, just to think about things. Let's find out where Flo's place is."

Wrapping up her takeaway in preparation for dumping it into the nearby rubbish bin, Ashley nodded, then climbed out of the car briefly. By the time she returned, she felt invigorated once again.

As Tim noticed the change in Ashley's demeanor, he smiled. Every time they'd worked on a case together, he'd found it difficult to watch as she'd had moments of struggle. He knew she wanted to be one of the best agents in the Bureau. He equally knew that she was hard on herself, not liking it much when a particular case proved more difficult than others.

"Are you finished yet?" Ashley asked him, forcing Tim to grin and purposefully take an exceptionally slow mouthful of food. She laughed at him. "Nice try. Dump it, and let's go talk to these sisters again."

Tim nodded and did what he was told. He loved food, but he loved his job more. He didn't mind at all when Ashley told him what to do either.

CHAPTER 47

After calling Amber and arranging a place to meet, Tim and Ashley met up with her in a local café during her lunch break.

"Hello," Amber said as she stood up from the table she'd chosen. Shaking the hand of each agent, she felt nervous. "Do you have news for us?" she asked.

Tim and Ashley sat down at the table and immediately ordered coffee from the nearby waitress.

"No, not yet. We would just like to ask you a few questions," Ashley said.

"Of course," Amber replied, nodding. "What can I help you with?"

Ashley watched the young woman. She knew Amber was closer to Flo's age than Kim. That made her hopeful that Amber was the sister most likely to know Flo's movements, or places that she liked to hang out.

"Do you know if Flo had anywhere that she went to, maybe to take some time out or to think about things?"

"I don't understand," Amber said, looking confused.

"We know when Flo left the Lo-Cost Supermarket on Friday morning, but we aren't sure she went home straight afterward," Ashley said. "Do you know what she might have done before returning home?"

Amber shook her head.

"No," she started to say. "She did have a thing about the beach, though."

"The beach?" Tim asked.

"Yes," Amber continued. "Whenever she used to get in an argument with Dad, she used to go to the beach and sit on the sand for ages. She used to call it her thinking spot, but she hasn't mentioned that for years. I don't know when she would have last done that - gone there to think, I mean."

"Do you think she needed a spot to go and think, now that she's a married woman and successful in her career?" Ashley asked.

Amber looked serious as she took a moment to consider the question.

"I think … I think that she did have moments when she had to cool down."

"Cool down?" Tim asked. "After … an argument with her husband?"

"Yeah, I think Daniel saying things that sounded like accusations used to upset Flo a bit," said Amber. "I know she turned up on my doorstep a few times, angry or sad about him implying that she wanted to be with another man."

"And did she, do you think?" Ashley asked. "Want to be with another man, I mean."

"No! Well, not that I know of, anyway," Amber replied. "I mean, there *have* been moments between them where I do think someone else might have walked away from that situation with a partner. Flo loves Daniel, though. Even with his insecurities, I do believe that she loves him very much. I can't imagine her wanting to be with anybody else."

"Right," Tim said. "Is there anything that you might have thought about, that you think might be beneficial for us to know?"

"No. I keep thinking about her all the time," Amber said as tears began to appear in her eyes. "I wish I knew where she was. I'm so worried about her. Kim is too."

"Well, hopefully we'll have some news for you soon," Ashley reassured her.

"Daniel doesn't even contact us, you know," Amber added. "I thought that after we gave him our numbers, he would call in at least once, even if just to ask if *we'd* heard from her, but he hasn't. I don't get him at all. Sometimes I wonder..." she said, her voice drifting off as she reconsidered whether to express her thoughts.

"You wonder what?" Tim asked.

"It's just that ... sometimes ... I do wonder if he does actually love her," Amber replied. "I mean, does he even miss her?"

"You don't think he does?" Ashley asked, watching as Amber shrugged her shoulders.

"I dunno. He married her when he certainly didn't have to. He's rich. He could've had anyone," Amber replied. "I know she wasn't the one to bring up marriage first, so he must have had some reason for making her his wife," she continued before pausing for a moment. "I don't know. Maybe it *was* love."

Tim found himself intrigued by the conversation. While almost everyone he and Ashley had spoken to had highlighted Daniel's issues with jealousy, the conversation with Amber was the first that had held the question of whether Daniel loved Flo or not.

As the conversation dried up, Ashley and Tim excused themselves and withdrew from the café.

"That's interesting," Tim said as they climbed into the car.

"What is?" she asked, starting the engine.

"She didn't even sound convinced that Daniel Sloan loved his wife. I haven't heard anyone present that view to us till now," Tim replied.

"True," Ashley agreed. "Amber was far more negative about Daniel today than others have been. Let's go to the beach she mentioned. Maybe we'll get lucky and find another security camera somewhere around there. It's not much to go on, but worth a try. If there's a chance Flo went there, even for just a few minutes alone before going home, we have to check it out."

CHAPTER 48

After parking in the beach parking lot and climbing out of Ashley's car, the two agents stood and just looked. Their hope of seeing some kind of security camera nestling on a power pole over the carpark was lost. There was nothing there.

They both looked further. For the most part, there was nothing in the area that appeared likely to have any kind of camera. That was until they both spotted what looked like a brand new home located a little way up the hillside on the other side of the road.

"What do you think?" Ashley asked.

Tim nodded as he looked at the house.

"I think that looks expensive enough that whoever owns it probably wants it as secure as possible," he said before smiling at her. "Only one way to find out."

They jumped back into the car and drove the short distance up the incline from the beachfront. Upon driving down a paved driveway, they were both happy to see a vehicle parked near the doorway.

"Someone's home," Tim said. "That's a good sign."

Upon approaching the doorway, a man in his mid-40s opened the door before they'd had a chance to even knock.

"Can I help you?" the man said.

Ashley held up her badge.

"Sir, I'm Special Agent Power, and this is Special Agent Moore," she said.

"Yes?"

"We're investigating a young woman's disappearance

and wondered if you might happen to have a security camera on your home that faces down towards the beach," Ashley continued.

The man looked at them, not entirely friendly but certainly more relaxed than he had looked moments earlier.

"I do," he said, opening the door wider. "Please come in and tell me what you need."

As the agents entered the home, Tim spoke up.

"Sorry, what was your name, Sir?" he asked.

The man turned and offered him his hand.

"William," he said as Tim fulfilled the handshake. "William Jones."

Ashley and Tim followed William downstairs to a lower level that appeared to be a large open space that was enclosed only on three sides. On the side in front of them was only limited wall space on either side of the large opening and no windows. Even though its ceiling was the floor of the level they'd just walked down from, the space had been set up as an outdoor garden area. Outdoor dining furniture, a barbecue area, and a wide plethora of edible plants and shrubs hid the background of concrete walls, floor, and ceiling.

"Wow, this is beautiful," Ashley said, impressed at the view that came from the space they were in.

"It is," William said as he looked at her and nodded. "It is the culmination of a lifetime of hard work by me and my wife. This is where we'll retire."

Through the outdoor space they walked until they came to a door. After watching William retrieve keys from his pocket, he opened the door and ushered both agents inside.

"This is my office. Let me turn this on," he said as he pressed the power button on a desktop computer tower. After a few minutes, he logged into the computer and pulled up the folder of security footage. "This is the view the camera picks up. It's not centered on the beach, but you can see the carpark area just up here in the top right-hand corner of the film."

Tim looked at the screen. The camera had been set up to monitor the lower yard of the property. It appeared unintended that a portion of the beach area was caught in the same view.

"That might be perfect, Mr. Jones," Tim said. "Is there any chance that you have footage from Friday a week ago?"

"Yes, I should do. I keep it for a month, just in case we were to notice anything missing at a later time," William replied. He looked at the calendar on the wall and scrolled down through files on the computer until he found the correct date. "This is it."

"That's wonderful. Can you please forward it to around 11am?" Ashley asked, receiving a nod in confirmation.

As the three of them looked on, it was only minutes of footage before they saw Flo's car turn up. Ashley felt her heart beat faster as she saw Flo climb out of her car and walk up to the safety barrier that separated the carpark from the beach.

"Is this what you wanted to see?" William asked, curious himself about whatever investigation was being completed that might require his security camera footage.

"Yes," Tim replied.

They watched as Flo smiled at someone or something out to the right. To their dismay, whatever or whoever she was smiling at was outside of the camera's view. Regardless, they continued to watch. Almost as if something had pulled Flo out of camera view, they saw her continue to grin as she walked to the right, leaving behind the safety of the security camera. A few minutes later, they saw a man appear, jump into Flo's car, reverse, and then pull out of the carpark altogether. Whatever had happened to the right of where Flo had parked, the agents had no idea of.

Ashley felt mixed emotions. On one hand, it was incredibly unfortunate and dismaying that Flo should have left the camera view and not returned. On the other hand, at least they knew of one more spot she had been, meaning one more piece of the puzzle was complete.

"Thank you, Mr. Jones," Ashley said quietly.

"Actually, before we leave, can you fast forward about an hour on that, Mr. Jones?" Tim asked, surprising Ashley. The look he gave her told her that there was something else to consider.

They watched as noon came and went. They then continued to watch until 1pm came and went. Apart from one car pulling up, and two young lovers getting out and sitting on the bonnet of their car for half an hour or so, there was nothing else that was seen. Finally, after the footage ran past 3pm on that Friday, Tim called it.

"That's fine. I think we've seen all that we needed to," he said to William. "Thank you so much. It is greatly appreciated that we were able to see this footage."

William stood and nodded as he ushered them out of this office again. As the three of them walked upstairs, he spoke.

"As I said, I keep security camera files for at least a month. If you need to see that again, or see anything else, please let me know."

Ashley shook his hand once they reached the home's front door.

"We will. Thank you," she said before she and Tim walked out and quietly made their way to the car.

"Well, that provided us with evidence of where Flo went after she bought her groceries, but it doesn't shed any more light on what happened to her," Ashley said.

"No, not exactly, but drive down to the carpark again. I want to see something," Tim said cryptically. "Pull in there so that the left side of the car is aligned with that rubbish bin."

Ashley did as he instructed. When she turned off the engine and looked at him, she could tell his mind was active.

"What are you thinking?" she asked.

Tim considered his thoughts and then spoke.

"We know that the guy who took Flo's car was beyond the camera view," he said, making Ashley nod. "We know from the camera footage that the far right of the view was right at this rubbish bin. That means that if the man who took her car was driving his own car, he had to have parked here."

Ashley looked over to the right side of the car.

"Yes, there doesn't appear to be room for a second vehicle to have parked between us and the barrier on that side."

"Right. And we didn't see a car reverse this way on the camera," Tim said as he used his hands to indicate movement towards the left. "That means the only way that the car could have reversed out was this way," he said as he used his hands to indicate movement to the right. "Therefore, he can only have driven his car in this direction."

Ashley considered what he said. As she did, Tim watched her face.

"I know you're going to pick this theory apart, Ash. Speak," Tim said.

"Well, I like the idea, and think you may be right. We did see the guy reverse and turn Flo's car on this angle, indicating he went that way, so it makes sense that if he were to reverse his car and go the same way, we should have seen that on camera too," she said before pausing.

"But?" Tim asked.

"Two factors come to mind. Firstly, he might not have had a car himself. He could have walked to the beach from any number of places around here," Ashley responded.

"True," Tim said as he nodded.

"The other possibility is that he didn't park right in the carpark. There is enough room on the edge of the road so that he could have just pulled up with his car facing the correct way already, without having to reverse."

Tim ran all scenarios through his mind before nodding again.

"Yeah, without actual footage showing us what happened, it's guesswork, unless there's somewhere else here that has a security camera pointing this way," he said as he got out of the car and looked to the left of the house they'd just been in. After a few minutes of gazing, he sat back inside the car. "I can't see anything that would have security up there. It's mainly grazing land for horses, by the looks of it."

"Well, we know when the car left here," Ashley said.

Tim looked at his notebook, studying the details he'd written down.

"Yeah, Flo arrived here at 11:20am and her car left at 11:36am."

"Right," Ashley said. "We also know when it arrived at the apartment carpark."

"Yes, it pulled into the apartment basement at 12:05pm," Tim replied as he began working through the time calculations. "So she was parked here for sixteen minutes before her car left, and it took twenty-nine minutes to get back to the apartment."

Ashley nodded and smiled.

"Buckle up, Timmy Boy. We need to do some drive timing," she said as she fastened her seatbelt once again and then started the engine.

Driving the most direct route between the beach and the apartment, Ashley monitored the streets for cameras. She was excited to see two on the route before they arrived at the apartment.

Looking at her watch, she was instantly disheartened.

"Too quick," she said, seeing it only had taken them

fifteen minutes to get from the starting point to the last.

"So, either whoever was driving stopped somewhere on the way, or he traveled a different way," Tim said.

Ashley took some time to consider and analyze what they knew, and what was a possibility.

"It wouldn't be a normal thing to do, to not only drive a stolen car through the main part of town but also park it, get out of it, and then return to it and drive it away," she said. "He'd have to be pretty stupid to do that."

Tim nodded.

"I agree," he said. "I think this guy would have taken the least used roads to get there."

"Why take it at all, though?" Ashley pondered. "Why not just leave the car at the beach?"

"It seems to me that whoever it is, they are very aware of our processes and how we would conduct our search for Flo," Tim said. "We might not like it, but this person has led us in a few different directions, just by the way he's done things."

"Hmm," Ashley responded. "Well, we know that Flo was smiling when she walked out of view of that camera. That tells us that she likely knows whoever it was. Maybe she *did* just run away with someone. Maybe they had a plan to meet up there so she could jump into his car and wait while he returned her car home."

"Yeah, but the groceries make no sense if that's the case. Why would she spend that money? To cover her tracks and make it look like an abduction when it wasn't?" Tim asked, at the same time shaking his head. "I don't like it, Ash. Something about that scenario still doesn't sit well with me," he said. "And how did the guy get back to the beach from the apartment? We still don't know that either."

"Maybe she picked him up in his car," Ashley said, her mind active.

Tim watched her face. He sometimes found himself almost lost when looking at her. On those occasions, it was difficult to concentrate on what he was meant to be focusing on.

"We know where the guy exited this apartment building," he said. "The service station camera picked up that exit point. Since we're already here, let's go around back and look around a wider area to see if there are other cameras that he might have walked past. Maybe we missed one, last time we were here."

"Good idea," Ashley agreed as she started the car once again.

Slowly, the two of them looked up at every lamp post, every exterior wall of every building, and inside the buildings they could see the interior of. It had been a long shot that there would be more security footage to see that would show the unknown man and the direction he'd gone. Knowing how unlikely it had seemed that they would find something, didn't stop Ashley and Tim from both feeling disheartened at the discovery.

"I don't think we're going to find anything more today, Ashley," Tim said to her. "Let's call it a day, grab something to eat, and go back to the motel. You know you think best when asleep," he said, grinning.

Ashley smiled at him as she nodded.

"How well you know me, Mr. Moore," she replied as they drove away.

CHAPTER 49

After sitting for a couple of hours in the shed at the back of his property, he took a moment to look at the time. He was expected somewhere in three hours. Despite wanting to just be alone with his own thoughts and not see or talk to anyone, he knew that wasn't possible. It was of utmost importance that while he was doing what he was doing, he acted completely normal in his day to day life. The thought of anybody noticing he wasn't his usual self was like a nightmare to him. Some people in his position would have been worried about getting caught, because of the thought of being convicted and sent to prison. For him, the concern about getting caught was driven solely by the thought that if he was, he wouldn't be able to watch her anymore.

Time was of the essence if he wanted to be at his next appointment on time. Staring at the computer screen, watching her face closely, he pushed the small button that he'd installed just under the front of his desk. As he pressed the button, he watched Flo's face soften, relax, and then fall slightly sideways, just as it had done each time he'd let the sleeping gas fill the coffin. In some ways, it was one of the most beautiful things he'd ever seen.

He was glad she hadn't had too many moments of what looked like extreme stress since he'd placed her in there. She seemed to move between panic and then resolution. He liked that word. Resolution. He looked up at his wall for a moment. Resolution of Happiness. The words sat there, staring at him. He grinned, remembering a very fond memory.

Abruptly he stood, breaking his thoughts free. There would be time enough later for him to ponder the memories he had about Flo. For now, there was something very important that needed to be done.

After assembling what he would need, and checking the monitor once more to ensure Flo was in deep slumber, he briskly walked out of the shed and into the woods. Quickly he rolled back the turf, pulled up the layers of heavy woolen blankets, and then opened the casket lid. It was the moment that he found the scariest, but also the most enthralling. The risk of her waking and seeing him was always there. He found that possibility a small slice of danger that made his heart pump harder. Every time, he wondered how she would react if she woke and saw his face. Would she be surprised? Really? Or had she perhaps known all these years just how he felt about her?

For a minute, he just looked at her. She was so lovely. Women had come and gone in his life since he'd first met her, but she'd always held a special place in his mind and his heart, throughout his interactions with all of them. There just wasn't anybody like her.

Breaking himself out of his distractive thoughts, he knelt on the ground and quickly assembled all that he needed to. It was time for her to be cleaned, to be moved, and to be fed. It had taken a considerable amount of research to figure out how he could keep her alive and healthy when she would spend so long in one position. The methods he'd learned had so far proven successful. She was getting enough food, hydration, cleaning, and movement in her limbs. She just didn't know it.

The ritual took only thirty minutes to complete. He knew that he had forty-five minutes between when she fell asleep from the gas, and when she woke up. It was enough time for him to do what he had to in order to keep her alive and well. It was also enough time to allow him to touch her, look at her, and quite simply *enjoy* her.

When thirty minutes had passed, he quickly kissed her on her lips, lay her back, closed the casket lid, and then piled on the blankets and turf once more. He didn't hesitate in the area after the last piece was complete. With urgency, he took his supplies back to the shed and took a seat once more so that he could watch her wake up. After seeing her in person, it was his favorite part of every day, watching her wake up, clean and nourished.

He smiled as she showed the first signs of waking up. She had a groggy look on her face, but it was serene. He wished she could always look that way. The life she lived wasn't always happy. It should have been. She deserved nothing less.

He sat and watched her for another fifteen minutes. It was long enough for him to be sure that she'd woken up, and she was fine. When he had that reassurance, he shut off his computer and went to look at the oxygen bottles located in a cabinet on the outside of the shed. On reading the gauges, he could see the tanks would continue to provide enough air to keep her breathing for two more full days. The thought made him smile. His treat for her was coming to an end. In some ways, he was sad about that, but he knew he couldn't keep her there forever, nor did he have any desire to. She was a great writer. She had yet to make her name known to the world, but he did not doubt that she would.

After looking at his watch one more time, he shut down the power in the shed and locked the door securely. No matter what, he couldn't be late. He had things to do and people to see.

CHAPTER 50

That evening, Tim walked quickly from his room to Ashley's in the motel they were staying in. He'd just answered a call that he'd found interesting. He had no idea what it meant, but something about it had left him wanting to share it with Ashley straight away.

As he knocked, his mind returned to the conversation he'd just had. The words were still replaying in his mind when the motel door opened.

"Hey," Ashley said, smiling at him. "What's up?"

"Can I come in?" Tim asked. Once inside, he turned to look at her. "I just received a call that was forwarded to me from Sarah."

"Oh?" Ashley asked, curious about what she was about to learn. "Something to do with the case? *This* case?" she asked, for a moment hoping she wasn't going to be taken off the case and sent away without solving it.

"Yes," Tim said as he sat down. "The call was from a woman who saw Flo's face on the news. She said that her husband is missing, and she thinks the two cases are related."

"Oh?" Ashley asked, confused. "How?"

"She told me that she met Flo briefly when she was on holiday with her husband in Paris," Tim replied. "Flo's friends and sisters all mentioned that holiday, didn't they? I recall them talking about it, saying that Daniel had been particularly jealous."

Ashley nodded.

"Yeah, but who's this woman, and who is her husband?"

"Her name is Barbara Brammell. Her husband's Tony Brammell. She said when she was introduced to Flo in Paris, Tony Brammell told her he'd been Flo's English teacher in high school," Tim said. "She reckoned there was something about Daniel that scared her when they met him and Flo on holiday. She's convinced that Daniel's taken her husband."

"Right," Ashley said. "Do we need to visit Mrs. Brammell then?" she asked.

"I told her we would go and talk to her first thing tomorrow morning," Tim said, nodding.

After doing some pacing as she tried to align the news with all they'd learned so far in the case, Ashley sat beside him.

"So this is yet another person who's mentioned the temper of Daniel Sloan," she said. "The way everybody has described Flo, she sounds like she's not at all aggressive. How did she end up with someone like him, I wonder."

"I don't know. All I can think about is finding her alive before it's too late," Tim said.

"It might already be too late, Tim," Ashley replied, her voice almost a whisper.

"I know, and now we might have a second person to try and find," Tim replied.

"What was the timeline with her husband's disappearance? Did she say?" Ashley asked.

"No, she was pretty distressed as she spoke," said Tim. "It was difficult getting anything out of her except those main details."

"Alright, well, that gives us something else to think about tonight, I guess. It would be a pretty big coincidence if Flo goes missing and then an old teacher of hers does too, especially when they recently saw each other on holiday in the same place, and this guy's wife has also mentioned how weird Daniel acted about Flo talking to the guy," Ashley said as she stood up and began walking toward the door. "Thanks for letting me know. I'll see you at breakfast."

Tim smiled at her sadly.

"Goodnight," he said before walking out. As if one mystery hadn't been enough, now they had another one to investigate.

CHAPTER 51

"Mrs. Brammell? I'm Special Agent Power, and this is Special Agent Moore," Ashley said as the front door opened at the address Tim had been given the night before.

"Oh, thank you for coming so quickly!" gushed the woman, obviously distressed. "Please come in," she continued, ushering Tim and Ashley inside.

"We understand that you think your husband is missing, Mrs. Brammell. How long has it been since you last saw him?" Ashley asked and watched as the woman before her sat down, visibly shaking.

"The last time I saw Tony was Thursday last week," the woman replied. "He had been here the night before, as he always was. The next morning, he got up and went to work, and I haven't seen him since. I've been calling his phone, but there's no reply."

"Have you called his work to see if he's been there?" Tim asked gently.

"Yes, of course," Barbara said. "I called Friday morning, because I didn't consider he was missing until then. He sometimes went out on Thursday nights, so it was only when I woke up Friday that he seemed gone."

"Where does he go on Thursday nights, Mrs. Brammell?" Ashley asked.

"I don't know," Barbara replied as she shrugged her shoulders. "I never asked. I think when any woman has a husband who doesn't tell her where he's going, the first thing assumed is that he's having an affair."

"And is he?" Tim asked. When Barbara looked at him

with a confused look on his face, he elaborated. "Having an affair?"

"Oh," Barbara began to reply. "I don't know. There have been times when I've thought so because he certainly goes *somewhere*."

Ashley looked at Tim. For a woman who was concerned about the whereabouts of her husband, Barbara Brammell suddenly looked remarkably calm.

"Pardon my saying so, but you don't seem at all worried about the possibility of that being a reality, Mrs. Brammell," Ashley said.

"No," Barbara said, a slight blush appearing on her face. "Tony and I stopped having … sex … a long time ago. When we met, it was different, but over the past few years, he just seemed to have stopped having any interest in it - well, with me anyway. I accepted it long ago, so have come to expect that he may be sharing that with someone else instead," she continued before pausing for a moment. "I do love him, and I do believe that he loves me. For that side of things, however, I don't seem to be what he wants, and I've just accepted it."

"Do you think there's a chance he's just gone off to be with someone else?" Ashley asked gently.

"I don't know," said Barbara. "That is what I would have thought until I saw that girl on the news - the one that's missing. Then I thought that maybe the two disappearances were related. It seems odd to me that we ran into her in Paris, and now she's missing, and Tony is too."

"Yes. Can you tell us, in what ways has your husband talked to you about Mrs. Sloan?" Ashley asked.

Barbara took a long moment to consider her reply.

"He didn't talk about her at all, but…" she said, then paused.

"But?" Ashley prompted.

"But after we'd run into her and her husband, Tony's demeanor did change," Barbara said. "He didn't use words to say so, but I could tell from his body language that he was ... energized, I guess would best describe it. It was like seeing her instantly woke him up."

"What do you think that signified?" Ashley asked.

Barbara looked thoughtful once again.

"I think it was just because he loves teaching so much," she said. "He does form good teacher-student relationships with the young people he teaches. Seeing them out and about in public always seems to give him a boost. I suppose that's because he loves his work so much. The young people are a big part of his life."

Tim and Ashley looked at one another. It was a great thing that Mrs. Brammell was so open and eager to talk, but both agents remained mindful of the time that continued to pass. No matter where questioning took them, always in the back of their minds was the hope that wherever Flo was, they could still find her alive.

"Mrs. Brammell," Tim said. "Is there any chance I could look around to see if there is anything in your home that might help us to know where to begin looking for your husband?" he asked.

"Oh, yes, of course," Barbara replied. "I looked through his things to see if anything was missing, but it doesn't look like it."

Tim nodded and smiled before walking out of the room, leaving Ashley in the living room with Barbara.

Walking from room to room, Tim had no idea what he was even looking for. He wasn't sure if Tony Brammell had disappeared in the same way that Flo had. He wasn't even sure if Tony Brammell had disappeared at all. It sounded more and more like he might have just shacked up with a woman he'd possibly been having an affair with.

On casual inspection, the main bathroom revealed nothing. The same was true of the three bedrooms - until Tim looked in the closet of one. On the left-hand side of the closet was something resembling a door, although there was no door handle. The only thing that made it look like it might be a doorway was a tiny keyhole that could easily be missed.

Tim pressed on the door, thinking it an odd place to have any kind of room. Feeling around the edges, there was no indication of any air flowing from it. Tentatively, he touched the lock. It was smaller than any lock he'd seen before, but he was pretty sure that was what it was.

Curious, he stepped out of the closet and returned to the living room.

"Mrs. Brammell, do you have a key for the door inside one of your closets?" he asked. The look he received told him that what he was referring to, the woman in front of him didn't seem to have any idea about.

"Door ... in a closet?" Barbara asked as she stood up, clearly confused. "I ... I'm not sure. Where?"

Tim led her and Ashley through the hallway and the bedroom.

"In here," he said as he pointed to the hidden door.

"Oh! No!" Barbara exclaimed. "I had no idea that was even there," she said. "Whatever it is, it can't be very big as the adjoining closet backs onto this."

On hearing her words, Tim took a mental note of where the doorway sat and then walked into the bedroom next door. Ashley followed him in.

"What do you think it is?" she asked as he glanced at her. The placement of one closet certainly was close to the other, but not quite perfect. Tim couldn't be sure about the alignment without opening the space up, or at least having a tape measure. Without either of those options, he guessed that there was a gap of almost a couple of meters between the closets, hidden within the walls.

"Hidden room," he said, smiling.

They moved back into the original room where Barbara still stood.

"I don't understand why I wouldn't know this was here. Now that you've pointed it out, I can see that's a keyhole, but I've never even noticed it before."

"You don't come in here often?" Ashley asked her.

"No, this is a guest room," said Barbara as she shook her head. "Tony always wanted to be responsible for this one because it's mainly his family that comes and stays with us. I've never questioned if there might be another reason he wanted to have control of it."

Tim felt restless. Behind the door, he knew there could be a space that would turn out to be an access point to plumbing or electrical cables, safely hidden out of reach. His gut told him it might be more.

"I can open this right now, Mrs. Brammell, with your permission," he said, knowing he always carried a lock pick set in his pocket just in case he ever needed it.

"Yes," Barbara replied easily as she nodded.

Ashley swiftly pointed out to her that she didn't have to grant them access. She had the right to say no.

"Thank you, but I am curious myself," Barbara responded. "I still can't believe that I didn't know this is was even here."

Without delay, Tim got to work. It was only a short time before he heard the lock click open. Immediately after hearing that sound, the door swung a few centimeters toward him. Even knowing it might be just a household maintenance cupboard, he felt his heart beat faster as he used his fingers to feel the edge of the door and pull it toward him.

To his surprise, there was no indication whatsoever that the space had ever been for maintenance. When the door was fully open, Tim felt around the edges until he found a small switch. When he flicked it, light illuminated a space that held a small desk with a compact computer on top of it.

"Oh!" Barbara exclaimed as she peered over Ashley's shoulder. She was so surprised by what the agents had found that she was quite speechless.

Tim discretely put on a glove from his pocket, reached forward, and touched the computer monitor. He was surprised and happy to find it a touch screen. As soon as the screen came to life, he saw footage that made his blood run cold.

Although she couldn't see the screen because of the way Tim was standing, Ashley could read his body language. Whatever he'd seen had made him tense up. She took the opportunity to usher Barbara Brammell away, reassuring her that whatever they found, they would let her know about.

Once Barbara was away from the closet area, Ashley moved forward until her chest met one side of Tim's back. She saw him briefly turn and look at her before directing her view to the screen.

"Is that…?" Ashley began to ask. She could see that it was Flo lying horizontally. She just couldn't quite believe it.

"Yep, that is definitely Flo Sloan," Tim said as he pulled out his phone. "We're going to need more help with this."

Ashley listened as she heard Tim make a call, requesting a crime scene investigator, or tech, or whoever would be best to analyze the computer, the room, and wherever the source of the footage was.

When he hung up the call, he turned to Ashley again.

"They're sending someone who can scan this room for evidence."

"Is that a recording, Tim?" Ashley asked as she turned her focus to the screen. "That time stamp…" she said, looking at her watch. "Reads now," she finished.

Coming to the same conclusion, Tim was horrified.

"We're watching Flo, where she is right now…" he said as his voice trailed off. "Shit, I hope these guys get here soon."

"Well, if that is happening right now, at least we

know she's alive. Her chest is moving," Ashley said. "Let's talk to Barbara some more. I think we need to know quite a bit more about her missing husband."

Reluctantly, Tim followed Ashley out of the small room, through the bedroom, and back into the living area. Once there, the three sat down.

"I don't understand any of this," Barbara said. "Is that something that Tony has been using? Why would he have a secret computer? We have one right there," she said as she pointed to a large desktop computer located on a table to the side of the living area.

"Mrs. Brammell," Ashley began. "Can you tell us exactly what happened in Paris when you saw Flo Sloan?"

Barbara looked confused but answered.

"We - Tony and I - were on a trip to Paris," she said. "We went to a flash restaurant. Actually, I think it might have been called a café, but to me, it was more like a restaurant. It's apparently well known as a place that some famous author or other used to spend time at. That appealed to Tony, of course, being the book fanatic that he is. Anyway, when we were walking in, Tony walked away from me and walked right up to this young woman. It was like he forgot I was by his side for a moment," she continued, with sadness on her face. "He introduced me to her. She seemed friendly enough, but then her husband came up to us. He made it very clear that they were married, and then he led her away."

"You didn't see her again in Paris?" Ashley asked.

"No," Barbara said, shaking her head. "We left the next day."

"How long was your trip to Paris, Mrs. Brammell?" Tim asked.

"Oh, only a few days. It was a lovely surprise from Tony," Barbara replied. "I didn't even know we were going until the morning of our flight."

Ashley and Tim looked at one another.

"Do you still have your tickets, Mrs. Brammell?" Ashley asked.

"Yes!" Barbara replied before standing, walking to a side unit, and pulling a small plastic ticket folder out of a drawer. "I always save my travel documents."

"Do you travel quite a lot? Is it usual behavior of your husband, to surprise you with a trip at the last minute?" Tim asked.

"Yes, and no. We used to travel a lot. These past few years, we haven't at all, but no, even when we were traveling all the time, we only ever did that with a lot of planning. He did surprise me with the short notice of this trip," Barbara replied as she handed the ticket folder to Tim.

Tim opened up the folder and looked through the pages inside. Everything had been purchased the night before the flight over to Paris. He made a mental note to ask Daniel Sloan when he'd planned and purchased tickets for the trip he and Flo had made. It was only a guess, but Tim considered that it might turn out that Tony had purchased tickets for him and his wife shortly after Daniel had done the same thing.

"Thank you," Tim said as he handed the ticket folder back to Barbara. "Mrs. Brammell, we are expecting a couple of our work colleagues to come here shortly to look at the room with the computer. Do you mind if we stay here until they arrive?"

"No," Barbara said. "Please do whatever you need to do to find Tony. I know he's not perfect, but I do love him."

Tim didn't correct her in any way. Knowing how distressed she'd been when they'd arrived, he didn't feel it right to tell a worried wife that he and Ashley were no longer considering her husband a missing person, but instead a suspect in their missing person investigation.

CHAPTER 52

Knowing that the hidden room was in the sound hands of professionals who knew what to look for not only within the room but also within the computer, Tim and Ashley waited. There had been reassurance that Flo Sloan had still looked alive when they'd seen her face on the computer screen. Seeing she was in a confined space had them both worried. It was entirely possible that there was a time limitation on getting her out before the air ran out.

As Mrs. Brammell made them cups of tea and brought out biscuits, Tim observed her. She was worried about her husband not having been at home in recent days. Tim suspected that the way she was fussing over him and Ashley was just her way of coping with concern. Neither agent had told her what exactly they'd seen on the computer. That news would come out at a later time. There was no need to distress her more in the meantime.

"Can you tell us a little about your husband, Mrs. Brammell?" Ashley asked.

Barbara looked up at her, tears evident in her eyes.

"Yes," she said. "What would you like to know?"

"You mentioned he regards young people highly in his job. Where does he work?" Ashley responded.

"Oh, he is a teacher at the local high school. He's been there for too many years for me to remember exactly how many. He loves it. He always has. The kids that pass through there are his life," Barbara said.

Tim was curious about the last statement.

"Do you think he sometimes regards the kids he teaches a little *too* highly?" he asked, wondering how she would respond.

"What do you mean?"

"I mean, he didn't see it as just a job that he did for those hours each day, and then switch off at night?" Tim asked.

"Oh, no! He was always talking about one student or another," Barbara said. "I don't take much notice of which young person he talks about, or what they've done to make him notice them so much. I just let him prattle on and on about them."

"And he hasn't been at work these last couple of days?" Ashley asked.

"No, that was the sign that told me something was really wrong," Barbara replied. "The principal contacted me and asked if Tony was at home. I didn't understand until he told me that Tony hadn't turned up to work. The principal sounded as worried as I am."

"We're done," one of the investigators said quietly to Tim when they entered the living area. "Do you want to talk about our findings here?" they asked.

Tim and Ashley stood abruptly.

"No," Tim said. "Do you have everything that you might need to help us find this person?"

"Yes, we won't need to come and see that again," the investigator confirmed.

Tim pulled himself away to go and close the door to the hidden room, taking time to replace everything as it had been. It didn't look as though Tony Brammell would be home anytime soon, but if he did make an appearance, Tim didn't want Tony to think his wife had found the computer.

"Thank you, Mrs. Brammell," he said as he returned to the living room. "We'll leave you now."

Barbara moved up to him, a look of desperation apparent on her face.

"Did you find something that might help find my Tony?" she asked.

"I am sure that we will find Mr. Brammell very soon," Tim reassured her. "In the meantime, could you please call me if he comes home?"

"Yes, of course," Barbara replied as she took his card.

"Oh, one more thing, Mrs. Brammell," Ashley said. "Can you please tell us the color, make, model, and license plate number of your husband's car?"

Barbara obliged as Tim wrote down the provided details into his notebook.

"Thank you," Ashley said to Barbara. "We'll be in touch soon."

The agents and investigators let themselves out and assembled near the vehicles on the roadside.

"Is there any way that you can find the location of where the girl is?" Ashley asked the investigator. "Did seeing the computer help at all in helping us find her?"

"It will do," the investigator replied. "I've taken some metadata from the camera feed. I have a few things to check and run through the system at our office, but I'm confident we can track where that feed is coming from. Give me a couple of hours. I'll let you know as soon as I have something."

Ashley let out a deep breath. It wasn't absolute, but at least it sounded positive. She held out her hand, grateful.

"Thank you."

"Don't thank me yet," the investigator said. "I am hopeful, but as you know, sometimes we just aren't able to get the answers we need."

Tim and Ashley moved away to sit inside Ashley's car.

"Well, it's sounding like we might be onto something. That's a good thing, Ash," Tim said. "I'll call this license plate number through now so the BOLO can go out," he continued before pulling out his phone and placing the necessary call. Just having the car details of the man who they now believed had taken Flo, was enough to feel positive about.

"Yeah, and we know now that it's most likely Tony Brammell that has her," said Ashley. "Let's go and do some investigating into his background," she said as she started the engine. "I wonder if there's anything in his past that could point us in the right direction to find out where he's holding her."

Driving away from the Brammell house, Tim thought about the wife inside. She'd seemed timid and honestly upset about the fact that her husband was missing. Tim had believed her in that, even though he accepted that she could have just been acting.

One thing Tim had learned long ago was that those that looked the weakest, often were actually master manipulators instead.

CHAPTER 53

"Right! Let's see what we can find out about Mr. Tony Brammell," Tim said as he sat at the small table in Ashley's motel room and opened his laptop.

After a few minutes of searching, Tim turned to Ashley.

"He doesn't have a record, but there's a load of news about him. Most of it's good news. This guy's been awarded for his teaching efforts heaps of times," he said. "All of this makes him look like an angel. It's hard to believe he's the same guy who might have abducted someone."

"You said *most* of it is good news," Ashley said. "What are the bits that aren't?"

Tim studied the text in front of him.

"Shit," he muttered.

"What?" Ashley asked him.

"Oh, sorry," Tim replied as he glanced up at her briefly. "So he, as an adult, is clean. There are no records on him for any offenses, but when he was a child, he was in the news."

"For what?"

"Get this," Tim said, reading ahead. "His mother was charged with child abuse."

Ashley watched him as he spoke.

"Did she beat him?" she asked and saw the look of horror that spread over Tim's face.

"No," he finally said, looking directly at her while shaking his head. "She was charged with … locking him in a wooden box. This says that she used it as a form of punishment. After she started doing it to him, he started acting out at school, beating other kids up. With every level of violence he delivered, his mother would force him into the box for longer periods of time."

"Wait, so she drove her own kid to anger and then violence through treating him like that, and then she punished him for increasingly longer periods because of it?" Ashley asked. When Tim nodded, she let out a deep breath. "Psycho bitch," she muttered under her breath.

Not used to hearing Ashley speak like that, Tim looked at her with surprise on his face.

"Sorry," she said. "You know me. When I hear about mothers treating their kids badly, it just makes me so angry."

"I know," Tim said, nodding. "At least now we know a little bit more about who we're dealing with. No matter if it *was* his upbringing that has driven him to want to do this, he is going to have to pay for what he's doing."

"I know," Ashley said, nodding. "Do you think she was buried?" she then asked out of context. When Tim looked up at her, she expressed her concern. "Flo looked like she was in a coffin. Did it look like that to you?"

"It did," Tim replied, his face grim. "We're going to find her, Ash. We're so close now. I'm sure of it."

Ashley hoped so. The thought of a young woman missing had been bad enough. The thought of Flo lying alive in a coffin in the cold ground was truly horrifying. It was something she'd read about in her case studies, but so far, she had never personally been involved in a case of someone being buried alive. Thinking about the possibility made her shudder.

"Are you okay?" Tim asked as he saw the shiver on Ashley.

"Yeah," Ashley replied as she nodded. "I just want to find her. I don't want us to fail in this."

Tim stood, walked to her, and gently hugged her.

"We aren't going to fail," he said. "As soon as we find

Tony Brammell, we'll be on the downhill slope to finding Flo."

Just then, Tim's phone rang. Ashley watched as he answered it, listened for several minutes, wrote in his notebook, and then hung up.

"Come on," Tim said, standing and grabbing his coat off the back of his chair. "We already have a response to the BOLO. Tony Brammell's car is sixty miles north of here."

Ashley didn't have to ask or say anything more. She grabbed her car keys and moved at the same speed Tim was moving. They were on the road within minutes.

"What else did they say?" she asked him as they began their journey to the coordinates Tim had been given. "You were on the phone for a while."

"They gave me details of several sightings of the car, from which they had formed a possible route that he's taken today," Tim replied. "We're going to get him."

Ashley smiled at him. It wasn't a happy smile, even though she wondered if it should have been. No, her smile was more of just hopeful reassurance.

"Let's just hope that he hasn't done the same trick that he did with Flo's car," Ashley said. When she sensed Tim turn his head to look at her, she glanced at him in return. "It could be a possibility, Tim. This guy had enough forethought to purposely set up Flo's car to be stolen so that we would waste time looking for the driver of it. It's perfectly feasible that he's done the same thing with his own car, and for the same reason."

"Maybe," Tim said. "Pretty soon, we'll know."

Two thirds into their drive north, Tim saw something that made him alert.

"Is that him?" he asked, looking at Ashley. "Can you see it?"

Ashley heard his words and didn't flinch. While maintaining her sight on the road, she saw the car Tim had referred to. It was at a service station. When both agents looked, they saw Tony standing at a pump, refilling his gas tank. Ashley drove past while keeping a cautious eye in her rear vision mirror.

"You don't want to stop?" Tim asked.

"No," Ashley replied. "He's walking into the shop now to pay. I'm going to pull over up here near this rubbish bin and see if he comes back this way again," she said as she edged to a stop in the small rest area. There was a chance that Tony would turn and begin traveling south again. Regardless of which way he went, they could discretely monitor his movements. "Got any rubbish?" she asked Tim as she unbuckled her seatbelt.

Tim smiled as he handed over wrappers from the last takeaway meal he'd eaten in her car.

"See, I knew it would be worth leaving these in here," he said, determined to get a smile in return.

Ashley grinned and began to climb out.

"You keep watching in the mirror."

She exited the car and moved slowly toward the rubbish bin. With the sun behind them, she raised her head toward it, looking as though she was taking a moment to enjoy it. Behind her sunglasses, she was actually watching Tony Brammell walk out of the service station, get back in his car, and begin driving toward the rest area.

That was all that Ashley needed to see. She moved in a relaxed manner toward her car. Just as she climbed in, she saw Tony's car drive past. Purposely, she let three cars pass before moving out onto the road again.

"Should we call for backup?" Tim asked. He loved how tough his partner was, but there were always times when a bit of heavy support was needed.

"I don't want to freak him out if he thinks cops are closing in on him," Ashley replied. "Put the call through that we're following behind him on this road, but tell them to hold back from doing anything yet. Let's tail him and see where he leads us, then call for help when we know for sure if Flo's there. It might be that we need to follow him somewhere else to find her, and that is what I'm most worried about."

"It's weird that he traveled south to the gas station and now is going back north," Tim said. "What's up with this guy? I mean, he's got a good life, a good job, a wife who obviously loves him, and no criminal record."

"That doesn't mean he hasn't offended. It just means he hasn't yet been caught," Ashley said, glancing at Tim briefly. "They all have clean records until the day their luck runs out."

"True," Tim conceded.

No more words were spoken for the remainder of their journey, each agent quiet in speech but busy in their own heads. Consistently, they remained behind one, two, or three cars that filled the gap between them and Tony's car. When the last gap-filling car veered off to a side road, Ashley slowed down, letting the space remain long between them and Tony.

"This is forest country," Tim said quietly as he looked on either side of the road and only saw trees. "That doesn't make me feel good."

"No, me neither," Ashley replied.

As the car in front of them slowed down and the right side indicator began flashing, Ashley and Tim watched as they saw Tony Brammell turn down what looked like a long driveway. Once he was out of sight, Ashley edged the car over to the roadside and pulled out her phone. Starting up her maps app, she took note of the GPS coordinates then turned to Tim.

"What do you think?" she asked him.

"We can't see anything from here, and we don't know what's down there," said Tim. "Ash, we need backup."

"Agreed," Ashley replied as she nodded. After making a call to request manpower come and support them, she started the engine. "Let's find somewhere out of sight to park. Who knows when he's going to leave again, and I don't want him to get spooked."

Quietly, she moved the car forward until, up the road further, they found a discreet spot to park and wait. In the silence of the car, Tim's phone ringing made both agents jump.

"Yep?" he said as he answered the call. "Are you sure?" he asked, then listened for a few moments longer as he indicated for Ashley to hand him the paper she'd written their current GPS coordinates onto. "Okay, thanks."

When he hung up, he saw Ashley's look of expectation.

"That was the tech investigator. They've worked their magic and are 99% sure that the coffin that Flo's in, is in there," he said, pointing toward the area that Tony had just driven.

"She's in there?" Ashley asked for clarification.

"Yep, looks like it. The investigator read their calculated coordinates to me, and they're identical to the ones that you wrote down," Tim said, his heart pounding. "What do you want to do? She's in there somewhere."

Ashley felt torn. She wanted to get to Flo as quickly as possible. The not knowing about how Tony Brammell was going to react, or even knowing what was down the driveway, was concerning. She took a few minutes to think.

"Vests on and phones on silent," she said abruptly. "Let's walk in there on foot but be prepared for anything. We can at least take it slow and just look around."

"Agreed," Tim said as he nodded.

Pulling their vests on and readying their firepower, Ashley and Tim slowly and carefully walked back along the road the short distance they'd traveled to park. Once at the beginning of the driveway, they took their time to slowly move down it, stopping every few yards to check in with each other via sight only and to just listen.

Aware that walking near forest area produced the potential for making sounds such as the crunch of twigs breaking underfoot, Ashley was nervous. It wasn't often that they went into remote situations blind, but not able to shift from her mind the images of Flo inside the coffin pushed Ashley to keep moving forward. She knew Flo had been alive when they'd seen her on the computer screen. Even so, there was no way of knowing how many hours, or even minutes, they might have until that oxygen ran out - if it hadn't already.

After a five minute walk up the driveway, they came to the edge of an opening that provided a view of an old homestead. Comprising two levels, the house looked abandoned. Highly run down, there wasn't anything about it that said it had been lived in recently.

From where they crouched behind some bushes, the two agents remained still and just watched. They could see Tony Brammell's car parked outside the front door. What they wanted to do was somehow get around the back of the house.

Using hand signals only, Tim and Ashley maneuvered themselves around one side of the home, taking their time to move through the tree line as silently as they could. It was a painstakingly slow process, but they remained hopeful they might see something worth the risk.

Bit by bit, they rounded the side of the house and found a sheltered spot to crouch down and watch the rear of the structure. It wasn't long before they saw Tony walk out the back door and down the steps into the yard. Remaining absolutely still, Ashley and Tim watched as Tony then walked a distance toward the tree line and entered what looked like a decent sized shed. Despite having the opportunity to approach Tony at that moment, Tim and Ashley remained where they were.

Another half an hour later, they saw the door of the shed open once again, and Tony walk out. This time, he walked around to their side of the shed, looked at tanks that were nestled up against the wall, and then began walking into the woods. They noted that in his hands, they could see two buckets. They were too far away to see what was inside either of them.

Seeing and taking note of the exact entry point into the trees that Tony went through, they watched until they couldn't see him through the growth anymore, then retreated. After the long slow process of making their way back to the road, they were greeted by a small SWAT team waiting in vehicles on one side. On the other side of the road was an ambulance.

Ashley felt relieved. She'd expected help to arrive in a matter of hours. She was pleased to find it had been able to be sent from a closer town a short distance north rather than from down south. Finally, they had the support they needed. They wouldn't have to keep Flo waiting any longer.

Before moving down the driveway again, a briefing was held. Tim and Ashley took time to describe all they had seen down the driveway and around the house. They detailed the shed that Tony had entered and exited while they'd watched. Despite knowing the two of them were also going to venture down there again with the team, they also described the point where Tony had entered the tree line.

Once ready, the group began the travel that would take them down to the shed and beyond. On arrival at the house, one man took up post directly at the front door. The rest moved around each side of the house. As always, Ashley fought to not be distracted by the incredible stealth such a team could work with while in dangerous situations. It was something she'd admired since the first time she'd seen a SWAT team at work.

Carefully, the team split up, with two entering the back door of the house and two more going with Ashley and Tim to look inside the shed. The entire room that they saw on entering surprised them, but Ashley moved directly to the computer monitor. On that, they could see the same camera feed she and Tim had seen at the Brammell household. Once again, the view they were presented with was that of the interior of the casket. Flo Sloan inside. It was a relief to see Flo's chest moving up and down.

They weren't too late.

CHAPTER 54

After his long walk down to the site where he'd buried the casket, Tony Brammell set up his gear and went through his ritual. He loved it so much. He loved *her* so much. He still had one more day to go until the oxygen tanks would become empty. He didn't mind. When Flo woke up, he knew she'd be pleased with what he'd done, because he'd done it for her.

He smiled to himself. Resolution of Happiness. That was the name of the outstanding essay she'd written in his class in her final year at high school. When he'd read it, his heart had soared. The skill that she'd shown in the formation of words was only highlighted by the passion she'd demonstrated in the content she'd written.

He'd often supposed that any student could have captured his heart through their writing. He was an English teacher, after all. Over his career, he'd read and marked hundreds of stories and essays. No, it was the way that she'd written about that particular subject that had secured his love for her. Maybe it was her writing that made his heart soar, but deep down, he knew it was also because he'd had similar experiences himself when he was young. Flo had perfectly expressed feelings that Tony had actually felt when he'd been put in that box as a child. Reading her words had made him feel like they truly were meant to be together.

Since the day she'd handed him that essay for marking, he'd probably read it thousands of times. The way she had talked about what it would be like to wake up in a coffin had been truly inspirational. She'd worded it exactly as she wanted it to be. He'd spent years considering her wishes and working to make sure he could do that for her, and do it right. Yes. With him, she would be pleased. That was the thought that kept him going. He'd watched her throughout her time with that idiot ex who had screwed around on her, treating her like she was worth nothing. More than once, Tony had wanted to kill that bastard. Instead, he'd forced himself to stay back, only watching and never actually entering Flo's life again in any way.

That was until he'd learned she'd gotten married. When he'd heard that, he'd initially been furious. She'd not only given her heart away, but she'd given it to that rich playboy who'd ended up treating her like she was his property.

Poor Flo. She never quite picked the right man. That was, until now, Tony Brammell told himself. He'd watched her wake up in the casket several times. Each of those times, he'd seen her smile and laugh. That was something he'd hardly ever seen her do when he'd watched her with the man who had so recently become her husband.

As he gently restored the casket lid then covered it again with the blankets and turf, he felt happy. It was the first time he'd truly felt that way in so many years. There had been a time when he'd loved Barbara, of course. She had suited him at the start. In more recent times, he had felt disconnected from her. He hadn't given her any thought at all when he'd begun planning for the experience he wanted to provide to Flo. He had even gone so far as to buy the house near the forest, purely so it would provide a quiet and private setting for Flo to lie peacefully.

Tony chuckled to himself. Barbara was so clueless that she didn't even have any idea that he'd sold the house he'd inherited from his grandmother two years earlier. That transaction had provided him with the money to buy the perfect house for his plan. It almost seemed like fate wanted him and Flo to be together. If that wasn't the case, why had everything slotted into place so perfectly?

Thinking about his wife again, he conceded that for someone else, Barbara was a good woman. For him, he'd just once again buried the woman he was meant to be with.

CHAPTER 55

Ashley directed the remaining SWAT team members to be ready when Tony walked back through the door of the shed. She'd considered them all going into the forest, but it was risky in case Tony ran while they were in there. With the computer monitor having been left on, and the lights running, Ashley was confident that he was going to return to the shed, even if only to turn everything off.

With a brief look around the shed interior, Tim's focus moved to a single tank that stood vertically underneath the computer desk. Quietly, he moved to it and read the label on it, noting its contents for when they would have time to look much closer at all aspects of the room.

They waited silently, positioned in preparation for the moment when Tony Brammell would walk through the door. When he did, he was forcefully dropped to the ground so quickly that he didn't even have time to realize what was going on.

Once they had him secured, Ashley began asking him where Flo was.

Tony only smiled.

"She's where she wants to be," he said cryptically.

They asked and asked. It was clear he had no intention of answering their questions, or revealing Flo's whereabouts.

"Take him out and tell the medics to come down here," Ashley finally gave as an order.

Once he'd been removed, Tim and Ashley looked

around the outside of the shed. Focusing on the external cupboard and the tanks that they'd seen Tony check earlier, they studied them.

"Oxygen," Tim said quietly. "That explains why she's still alive," he continued as he let his fingers follow the tubing coming off the tanks. On pulling it, he realized it was buried only an inch or so underground, leading in the direction where they'd seen Tony go when he'd entered the forest. "This way!" Tim yelled to the team around them.

As he walked, Tim continued to pull up the tubing. He was surprised by how far it led them into the trees before it seemed to be not able to be pulled anymore. He looked at Ashley, then at the ground.

The solid rectangular outline of a cut in the turf was obvious. Tim knelt and began investigating the grass area. Once he pulled a little, the entire rectangle of turf lifted easily. Underneath, he found woolen blankets and roughly threw them to the side. Finally, the casket was in view.

Abruptly, he and Ashley both lifted the lid just as the medics came forward. All were animated in uncertain suspense as Flo came into view.

"Move aside," one of the medics called out.

Without objection, Ashley and Tim retreated and then watched as Flo was checked over in the casket. Once Ashley had taken sufficient photos of each aspect of the casket and Flo lying in it, the medics carefully moved Flo onto a stretcher.

"She's alive, but in a heavy sleep," one medic confirmed to Ashley. "Let's get her into the ambulance," she instructed her teammates.

"Wait," Tim called out to the medic before they left. "Inside the shed, there's a tank you might want to see. I think it might be what he's been using to put her to sleep."

The medic nodded and walked inside the shed. She

immediately saw the tank and moved to ascertain what it was.

"If he's been sending that through to the coffin, Flo is one lucky girl. Too much of that, and he could have put her to sleep permanently."

Tim watched the medic walk out, shaking her head.

"I'll call you when the victim is secure in the hospital," she called out before leaving the shed to join her crew.

CHAPTER 56

After Ashley called in that they had Tony Brammell secured, and she'd received confirmation that a crime scene unit was on its way, she and Tim took their time to look more closely around the interior of the shed. The walls were covered with multiple copies of handwritten pages blown up to poster size.

"What is all this?" Ashley asked.

"I don't know, but look," Tim replied as he pointed to the name on one of the sheets of paper. "This was written by Flo."

"So was this one," Ashley responded as she looked at a different page. "He's blown up these documents to this big size. Why?"

"So he could read them easily while sitting at the desk and watching Flo, I imagine," Tim said as he focused on one page in particular. "Resolution of Happiness," he read out loud. "Geez, read the content of this one, Ash."

Ashley looked at the copy of the same report that was closest to her.

"How would I feel if I woke up in a coffin?" she read out loud. For the following few minutes, she read silently. "Do you think this is why he focused on her?" she asked Tim when she'd reached the end of the pages.

"Maybe," Tim said as he nodded. "Either that or it's one big coincidence. We know that his mother locked him in a wooden box when he did something she didn't like. Maybe when he read this, something clicked inside of him that made him feel like he and Flo had a special connection."

"I can see how that would be," Ashley said, nodding. "She's written this as if it would be almost a romantic thing, to wake up in a coffin. Look at the red lips on the corner of the pages. It looks like she kissed the report purposely with red lipstick."

"I can't even imagine how she affected Brammell if he read these words and could see that kiss on the page, having experienced what he did in his childhood," Tim said as he nodded.

"She was a teenage kid. She probably didn't even think anything about it. Nobody would expect their teacher to react to a simple report like this guy has," Ashley said, thoughtful. "I wonder if she even remembers *writing* this if she did it while at high school."

They continued to look around, remaining careful to not touch anything. It was a grim but masterful setup.

"I've never seen or even heard of anything like this," Ashley said. "He's actually got a to-do list here. It details everything including checking the gas and oxygen cylinders, digging up turf and blankets, washing her, moving her, and making sure her body is fed and hydrated. He had it all so well planned out."

Tim approached her and looked over her shoulder at the checklist on the wall.

"He's even marked off the days and times that he's done each thing," he said. "That'll definitely make charging him easier."

"But what was his end plan? I've heard of people being buried alive, but they've been left to die like that. This guy has been working so hard to keep her alive," Ashley said.

"Yeah, my guess is that he's been so obsessed with that report that he's decided to make it come true. As you said, Flo made it sound almost romantic in her writing. Maybe he's taken her words and those kiss imprints as literal, and he's put all this in place so she could have her dream come true."

Ashley shuddered. If that was the case, it had been a risky endeavor. If anything had happened to Tony and the oxygen had run out without anybody knowing where Flo was buried...

"Hey, we found her, and she's alive," Tim said, sensing the tenseness in his partner's body. "The crime scene guys will be here soon. Once they arrive, we need to get to the hospital and see if we can talk to Flo."

"Yeah, we need to get Brammell into interrogation, too," Ashley said. "I want to get straight onto getting this guy locked up so he can't do this again." When she'd remained silent for a few minutes, she looked at him. "You don't think there are other girls out there somewhere who have suffered this same fate, do you?" she asked.

"By him, do you mean?" Tim asked for clarity. When Ashley nodded, he replied. "The tech guys said they didn't find any trace of any other camera feeds, so no, I don't think so. I think that report may be the sole reason he did this to Flo."

"Yeah, but Tim, whenever Flo wrote that report, it's highly probable that the entire class had to write one on the same subject," said Ashley. "There could be another thirty people out there..."

Tim listened to Ashley speak, and her voice drift off to silence.

"Let's see what we can get out of him when we question him," Tim finally said. "Until then, there's no point guessing. If we're lucky, this guy is going to be crazy enough to talk himself right into a long term sentence."

"We need to let Daniel know," Ashley said, finally remembering Flo's husband. She pulled out her phone and rang his number.

"Hello?" he asked, desperation in his voice. "Flo?"

"No, Mr. Sloan, this is Special Agent Power," Ashley began to reply before being cut off.

"Have you found her? Oh my god, is she…"

"Mr. Sloan, we have found Flo. She is now on her way to Middlemore Hospital," Ashley informed him.

"She's okay?" Daniel asked. "She's … alive?"

"Yes, she is, but she was heavily sedated."

At the end of the line, Ashley could hear the same heavy weeping she'd already heard on several occasions.

"Thank you. I'll go to her now," Daniel said between sobs before hanging up the phone.

When the call disconnected, Ashley looked at Tim.

"If he isn't a distraught husband, he is a very good actor," she said quietly. "Maybe we've been wrong about Daniel Sloan all along."

Tim looked at her with a raised eyebrow.

"Maybe about his involvement in all of this, but in my view, he still doesn't deserve an award for Husband of the Year."

CHAPTER 57

As Flo was being carried toward the ambulance waiting at the top of the long driveway, she started to regain consciousness. At first, she felt almost blinded by the light. She moved one hand up to her eyes quickly, shading them.

"You're going to be alright now, Mrs. Sloan," she heard a woman's voice say. It sounded soothing. "Keep your eyes covered for the moment. You've been in the dark for some time. It'll take time to adjust."

"Where am I?" Flo asked, her voice groggy.

"We'll talk soon," the medic reassured her. "You're safe now. Soon we'll be on our way to the hospital so you can be fully checked out. For now, just rest and enjoy the ride," Flo heard the friendly voice say as she felt herself raised into the ambulance.

The sound of the ambulance doors closing startled her. Then she heard nothing more as once again, she fell into a deep sleep.

Although it was late by the time the property was secured and crime scene investigators had taken over the scene, Ashley was eager to talk to Tony Brammell. She just couldn't shake the fear that Flo wasn't the only young woman he might have abducted.

"It's getting late, Ash," Tim said gently, providing a voice of reason in what already seemed like an excessively long day. "Brammell's already on his way to security, and you and I have to drive south again, remember."

"I know. I just want to make sure he doesn't get away

with what he's done," Ashley said as they climbed into her car.

"He won't. There's no way he could, with all the evidence that's here and at the other house," Tim replied. "Come on. Let's get back to the motel and have a good sleep. There will be plenty of time tomorrow for questioning."

CHAPTER 58

Flo next woke up to see light again. This time, it was streaming in through a window. Although the light seemed harsh on her eyes, the feeling of warmth on her face was soothing to her.

As she slowly regained consciousness, she heard a familiar voice call out.

"Flo! Oh, my beautiful wife!" Daniel exclaimed as he moved quickly to the bed. He took her hand in his and raised it to his lips.

When she finally opened her eyes, Flo moved her head toward the voice and saw Daniel. Her instant reaction was to try and move away from him, pulling her hand out of his.

"Flo? What is it?" Daniel asked, his voice desperate.

"Mr. Sloan," Ashley said as she and Tim entered the hospital room. The reaction they'd seen from Flo towards her husband had been interesting, to say the least.

When they saw Daniel turn toward them, Ashley spoke again.

"We just came by to see how Flo is doing," she said as she moved closer to the bed. "Can we have a couple of minutes with your wife, please?"

Daniel was reluctant to leave.

"She's only just woken up," he said. "Can't you see she's not up for questions right now?"

Ashley stepped forward.

"We won't take up much of your time, Mrs. Sloan," she said, addressing Flo. "I'm Special Agent Ashley

Power, and this is Special Agent Tim Moore. May we speak to you briefly?"

Flo watched the interaction and nodded at the woman speaking to her. It was reassuring that law enforcement was there to protect her from the monster that her husband had turned out to be.

Tim prompted Daniel to leave the room with him, leaving Ashley and Flo alone.

"You've had quite an ordeal," Ashley said. "I know it's probably confusing to you, waking up here after all that you've been through."

Flo watched the woman and nodded.

"He did it. My husband did this to me," she said, panic in her voice.

Ashley shook her head.

"No, Mrs. Sloan," she said. "I do believe that your husband, throughout this, was grieving for you."

"But he … I woke up in a box … a coffin?" Flo tried to articulate.

"Yes, but we don't believe it was your husband who put you there," Ashley said, giving Flo a moment for the information to sink in. "Do you know Mr. Tony Brammell, Mrs. Sloan?"

Flo was confused.

"My old teacher from high school?" she asked. When she saw Ashley nod, she felt even more perplexed. "What does he have to do with this?"

As soon as she asked the question, fresh with Tony Brammell's face in her head, she remembered. Her mind processed the memory before she voiced what had come to mind.

"He … he was at the beach," she said. "I pulled over there to watch the ocean just for a few minutes before I was going to go home. I saw him there, in the carpark."

Ashley nodded but said nothing, letting the young woman find her way in her recall of the day she'd gone missing.

"I went over to say hello to him. I don't remember what happened after that," Flo said. "Then I woke up…" she started to say before breaking down into tears.

"You're safe now, Mrs. Sloan. Mr. Brammell is in custody, and I have no doubt that he will be charged. He won't be seeing sunlight again for a long time," Ashley said, hoping nothing would go wrong with the case once it went through the system.

"Daniel … didn't have anything to do with this?" Flo asked.

"No, not that we know of," Ashley replied. "Everything points to Tony Brammell, and *only* Tony Brammell."

Flo looked at the agent in disbelief.

"I thought it was him - Daniel," she said quietly as tears continued. "How could I have thought that about my own husband?"

"Don't distress yourself," Ashley said. "What you've been through may take quite some time to process and heal from. That's the most important thing now - that you get better."

Flo nodded but said nothing.

"I won't take up any more of your time now, but I might come and see you again in a few days, just to see how you're doing, if you're okay with that?" Ashley asked and saw the young woman nod in reply. "Would you like me to tell your husband to come in now?"

After a long moment of silence, Flo finally nodded. Thick in her mind was confusion, but she'd seen the badge of the agent. She had to have faith in what she'd been told. Daniel wasn't the one who had done such a horrible thing to her after all.

When he re-entered the room, the first thing she noticed about him was the degree to which his eyes were red and puffy. She'd never seen him cry at all. He looked like he'd been crying for days. Looking at him in those first moments of wakefulness, she felt mixed emotions.

"I'm so sorry," Daniel said as he stepped forward and sat on the edge of Flo's bed. "I've let my pride and my insecurity ruin what we have. If I hadn't started that argument, maybe none of this would have happened."

Flo studied his face and his countenance. His eyes were downcast. His facial expression was one of misery. It would have been so easy for her to end their relationship at that moment. Instead, with all that she'd been through, she chose to look at him with compassion.

She reached out her arms, welcoming him to move forward and embrace her. After a moment of hesitation on his part, he did.

"The agent that was just here said that it was an old teacher of mine that did this, Daniel," Flo said. "It didn't have anything to do with you or the argument we had that morning."

Flo held him close to her as she felt his body slump against hers. Usually presenting the image of a man of strength, he crumpled as he openly wept.

Her mind considering options, Flo knew she couldn't make any decision in her present state. Their marriage was something that needed work, but it wasn't the right time to walk away.

"I've located a shrink who I've already had an introductory session with. He's sure he can help me," Daniel said as he gently pulled away and rubbed his eyes. "I don't want to be like this forever, and I don't want to lose you or what we have. These demons inside of me, that make me react to you talking to men, need to be addressed and dealt with."

Flo nodded. She certainly agreed with that.

"They do," she replied. She had no idea if her husband did truly believe he needed help. She had no idea if resolving his issues would make things better between them even if he *did* get help. The only thing she was certain about was that she wouldn't walk away from him yet.

CHAPTER 59

"You look tired," Special Agent Tim Moore said to his partner as they prepared to return home. They were at their motel, loading their overnight bags into Ashley's car.

"I am," Ashley replied as she moved to climb into the driver's seat. Once they were both seated and buckled up, she spoke again. "This has been a strange case."

"Yeah, it has been a first for me," Tim agreed. "I'd never heard of anyone keeping someone alive in a coffin like that. And the freaky thing about it? The degree to which Brammell went to *care* for her while he had her confined."

Both thought about the interrogation they'd put Tony Brammell through. It was a rare case in which it would be surprisingly easy to move toward a conviction. During his questioning, he hadn't even tried to deny what he'd done to Flo Sloan.

"I know," Ashley said. "When he was talking about his daily rituals of washing her and feeding her to keep her healthy and nourished, I almost felt ill," she continued. "What surprised me was the way he sounded when he talked about it. I think he truly believes that he was making a dream of hers come true, and that he loves her."

"Weird kind of love," Tim responded. "The medics said the amount of gas he'd administered to Flo to make her go to sleep was extremely close to fatally dangerous. If he'd calculated incorrectly, he could have killed her."

"I guess his idea of love was different from yours or

mine. That isn't surprising, given what we learned about his childhood," Ashley said. "I mean, what kind of mother puts her kid in a box for hours on end? With the years that Tony was subjected to that, he could have gone on to do much worse."

Both remained quiet for some time, thinking about all they'd seen, heard, and learned during their time on the case. It was always the way with them. Debriefing and dissecting details of a case when on their way back to their normal lives was something that had developed into a routine for them.

"At least we know that Flo was the only one," Tim said. "It wasn't the scenario that made him want to take a young woman and put her through what he did."

"True," Ashley agreed, nodding. "The subject was intriguing to him because of his history, but it was Flo's report that affected him. I still can't understand why nobody at the school thought anything was abnormal about him."

"Whatever was lurking in the depths of that head, he hid it well. Everyone we've spoken to about him has said he's a nice guy and a great teacher. There haven't been any reports about bad behavior towards students or anyone else," Tim replied. "If I hadn't seen everything with my own eyes, I would have found it difficult to believe he would do that to someone."

"Well, like you said, he wanted to care for her. In his view, he was only giving her what she wanted," Ashley said. "I don't think he had some random need to bury someone."

"Well, he won't have the opportunity to now," Tim said before closing and changing the subject. "Hey, when can we stop and get coffee?"

"Just coffee? Sure," Ashley teased, grinning at him.

Tim laughed softly.

"Yeah, okay, and some food too?"

Several hours later, Ashley maneuvered her car up to the curb outside Tim's apartment. Having stopped for a relaxed meal midway on their way home, they'd said little since.

"Okay," Ashley said as she stopped the car and turned to look at him. "You have a good afternoon, and I'll see you back at work."

Tim heard the abruptness in Ashley's voice. Whenever they finished a case, he felt the need to talk to her about more personal things. Over their time working together, he'd learned that was something she didn't particularly want to do when they'd finished a case. On occasion, he'd tried to encourage her into a conversation, but decided not to at that moment. He was tired, and so was she. It was better to let things lie. The way he felt about her could wait in silence for another day.

Quietly, he watched her for a couple of minutes, thoughtful. Before his emotion got the better of him, he forced himself to grin at her.

"Thanks. You have a good afternoon too, Ms. Power," he said as he opened the door.

Ashley smiled and pulled the latch to open the boot of the car. She remained where she was as Tim closed the passenger door, went to the boot, and retrieved his overnight case. Before she pulled away, Ashley saw him grin and wave at her. In response, she tooted the horn briefly and began to veer away.

When she reached her home, Ashley moved through her usual routine of dumping her bag and letting herself lie down and completely relax. She always needed to be alone after a case was completed. Although she never felt physically affected when she was working, the depth of thinking they constantly did when on a case always seemed to result in physical exhaustion when it was over.

Lying down on her bed, fully clothed, she smiled to herself. She was glad that Tim hadn't tried to have a serious conversation when she'd dropped him home. As she thought about how she'd almost come to expect him to do it every time now, she realized that it felt odd to have him *not* having said anything.

Sleep took over. She felt exhausted but happy. Another case was over with, and a victim had been saved. Now she could relax - at least until the next case began.

~~~~~~~~~~~~~~~~~

The End
~~~~~~~~~~~~~~~~~

OTHER BOOKS
BY
ANN M PRATLEY

A POWER MOORE INVESTIGATION TALE
HOONIGAN
ANN M PRATLEY

HOONIGAN

Tristan Clarkson has woken up, over and over, bound to
a chair and unable to see. He has no idea where he is, or
why he is in the situation he's woken to. His memory is
vague, protecting him from recent events that will
eventually haunt him for the rest of his life. He wants to
remember, but at the same time his mind acts as though
he really, really doesn't. Initially, he's confused. With
each waking, his memory clears that little bit more, as
do his senses. He soon becomes aware that the very
person who has abducted him, is in the room with
him, determined to make Tristan pay for
something he can't even remember.

Meanwhile, in a hospital nearby, a patient has been
taken. With the help of Special Agents Ashley Power
and Tim Moore, an investigation begins into where the
man has been taken, and who would have reason to
remove him. With the patient having already been
weak from time in a coma, time is of the
essence in finding him alive.

Hoonigan is a blend of crime and suspense, intermingled
with the strength of friendship, and the awakening of one
father's realization of just how much his
son really means to him.

A POWER MOORE INVESTIGATION TALE
HOME BY THE SEA
ANN M PRATLEY

HOME BY THE SEA

A decade ago, homeless people began disappearing from
four neighboring towns. Day to day, the commuters
making their way to and from work never took notice of
the less fortunate they passed. They didn't notice as the
number of homeless reduced. They didn't even notice
when entire groups of homeless people vanished.

A young woman, eager to find out where her grandfather
disappeared to, began trying to find him. When four
police departments dismissed her, telling her that her
grandfather would no doubt turn up when he
wanted to, she was too young to realize
she should pursue the matter further.

Now, ten years on, she's stepped up and pushed harder
for something to be done to find not only her grandfather
but also the countless other people who seemed to
have disappeared around the same time.

Called in to investigate the disappearances, Special
Agents Ashley Power and Tim Moore find themselves
searching for - and finding - so much more than
they thought they would.

A POWER MOORE INVESTIGATION TALE

TIGER
IN OUR
HOUSE

ANN M PRATLEY

TIGER IN OUR HOUSE

When Alana Templeton goes to do the simple task of
hanging her laundry outdoors, she becomes aware that
something is not as it should be in her yard. The sound
she hears is one that many people might not recognize
at first. For Alana, it is, surprisingly, a sound
she's heard before.

Being in the yard, with her toddler in the doorway of
their home, she knows the right thing to do is whatever
she can to save him. The previous time the animal came
to their home, she succeeded, but will she this time?

A woman and her infant being put in danger of being
attacked by the large animal that has escaped the local
wildlife park, prompts an investigation into whether
there might be more than just bad luck behind the two
events. It seems unlikely that someone could have
used such a beast for an attempt on someone's life.
Then again, it seems unlikely that the animal would
escape its confine and end up at the same
location two times in a row.

Called in to figure out what might be behind the strange
occurrences, Special Agents Ashley Power and Tim
Moore begin to delve into an elaborate and rather
unconventional scheme to hurt someone
through an act of revenge.

.

FORBIDDEN CONFLICTS SERIES

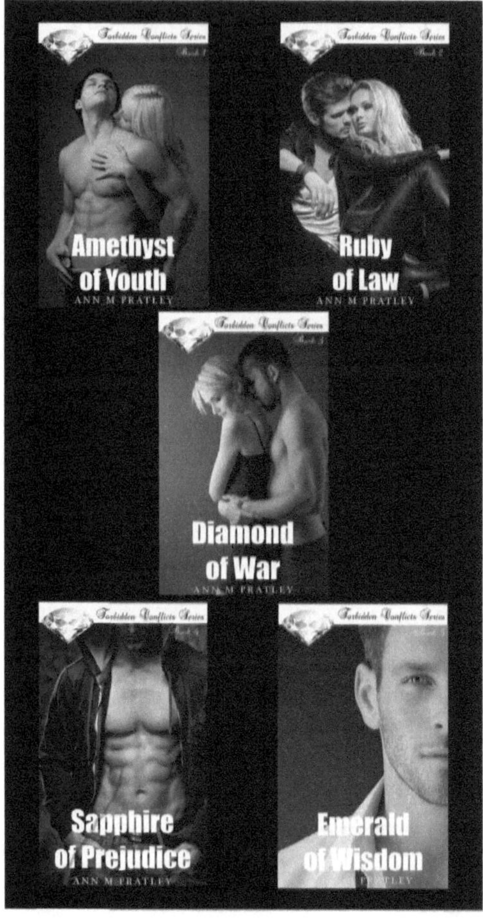

Crime Families ~ Passion ~ Suspense

AMETHYST OF YOUTH
(FORBIDDEN CONFLICTS SERIES - BOOK #1)

The youngest member of the Stonewarden family, Charlotte (Charlie), is 18 years old. As with everyone in her family when they reach that age, she's been told that when she turns 19, she'll be recruited into the family business. She has her warning that she has one year to do anything else she wishes to do - travel, study, work. Whatever she wants to do, she has 365 days to do it. On her next birthday, her life will effectively stop being her own.

But Charlie wants nothing to do with the business. The youngest of six, with five older brothers, she wants a different life. Maybe if the family business was something normal like a retail shop or a business centered around trade, she'd feel differently. There are people who say that her family's long term history of robbing from the rich and providing to the poor is a good thing. To her, all she can see is that they are thieves. Plain and simple.

Her view is further secured when she and her older brother, Max, are shot at in a local supermarket. Seeing Max lying in blood and later lying unmoving in hospital in a coma, pushes her further in her resolve to find a way to not take part in the activities of her father and brothers.

At the shootout, she is saved by a checkout operator, Ash. Whilst building their friendship, Charlie will learn things about her family that she didn't particularly wish to know. She will hear more and more that she can't share with Ash, and the more she learns, the wider the gap will become.

In years she's young, but having lost her mother when she was only nine years old, Charlie has an older soul. The possibilities she'll be presented with during her one final year of her own, will push her in her considerations of how she really wants her life to be. She wants one thing. Her strict ex-military father wants another. The dynamics of her new friendship will pull her in a third direction.

How will she chose what's right for her? And what would she have to do to break free from the chains that she can see her father wants to place around her for the rest of her life?

REVIEWERS SAY:
"This was a good clean romance with plenty of action to further the story along ... will make you ponder about life's situations, their actions and reactions, and how the decisions of past generations can affect the current ones. You'll be glad you read it!"

"... loved this book! It took me by surprise--great from start to finish! I don't normally read crime family dramas, but I love NA/coming-of-age novels. Charlie is on the cusp of being inducted into her family's Robin Hood-esque biz, but she doesn't want that. She isn't sure what, exactly, she does want...just not THAT. Her connection with Ash furthers that disconnect, and they stumble through the beginnings of young love together. Of course, secrets and family craziness threaten their romance at every turn. ...It's an awesome start to the Forbidden Conflicts series!"

"A wonderful read. A timeless push and pull between our own wants and our family's wants. Will she follow the path her family wants or will she follow her own path? Read the book to find out."

RUBY OF LAW
(FORBIDDEN CONFLICTS SERIES - BOOK #2)

For generations, the Leadbetters have lived off crime.
For as long as any of them know, fathers and mothers
have taught sons and daughters how to succeed in the
criminal world, primarily through theft.

Phillip Leadbetter is 29 and has devoted his whole life so
far to doing what his father and mother have told him to
do. The sacrifice for doing that is that he still lives at
home, not having yet met anyone who he believes could
accept the man that he is, because of his family.

One night, a potential tragedy brings him into the path of
Daisy, an up and coming professional in the legal sector.
Seeing him as her knight in shining armor, she can't stop
thinking about the rugged guy who saved her. She's also
very pleased when fate brings their paths to cross again.

Getting to know one another, both leave out major
details about who they are. She doesn't want him to
know she's a lawyer because some people just don't like
lawyers. He doesn't want to tell her about his family
and their long history of criminal activity.

How, then, will things turn when they meet up in a
courthouse, each learning in that moment who the other
really is? How will they deal with the fact that she is
on one side of the law, and he is very
definitely on the other?

DIAMOND OF WAR
(FORBIDDEN CONFLICTS SERIES - BOOK #3)

James Stonewarden is a playboy. He has been since the moment he first started to notice girls. He loves them all, and they all love him. Why would he want to get himself into a relationship?

Sasha Leadbetter's a hot-headed young woman, known to the law for her quick temper and harsh ways. She isn't one to mess with - especially with the way she keeps a blade in her pocket. To her, it's her security. It's something that makes her feel safe and comfortable. She's had it for so long that it's nothing for her to pull it out and hold it to someone's throat without any conscious thought.

Unaware of who each other are, or how their families are distantly interconnected through crime, the chance of James Stonewarden meeting Sasha Leadbetter is slim. But it happens.

A playboy, and a young woman who has the mentality to kill. What kind of recipe could that result in? And what will happen when James identifies a car at Sasha's family home, that matches the description his sister Charlie gave after the supermarket shooting months earlier?

SAPPHIRE OF PREJUDICE
(FORBIDDEN CONFLICTS SERIES - BOOK #4)

Greg and Rhett. They've grown up together since they were teenagers. They've fought together. They've stolen together. They've even loved women together. But something deeper has existed in one of them for years. He's hidden it well. Being part of the great Leadbetter gang and family, the prejudice toward certain situations has always been loudly expressed by many of its members - too many, and certainly enough to make anyone fearful of what would happen if feelings were revealed and brought out into the open.

A night has passed when finally, in a moment of wondering if he'd survive till morning, Rhett's taken the chance and kissed the person of his desire. Given their circumstances, what can they do, and where can they go?

Meanwhile, as Phillip Leadbetter continues on his path of happiness with his Daisy, someone from her past has grown obsessed with her and wants her back. To what degree will he put into effect a plan to get her back, and get Phillip out of her life forever?

~~ NOTE: This book does contain adult sexual content and LOTS of swear words.

* 9 7 8 1 9 9 1 1 6 4 6 3 6 *